Irgo Winfred Dane was the finest bass player in the town as something of a genius you make allowances, in my book. "You sat in once with my band—back in the old days," I said. I rubbed my face. "What kind of help were you looking for exactly? This is a police case."

"They only think of my niece as another dirty street person. But she was just a little girl. What would make a person do something so horrible to a little girl?"

"I don't know, Mr. Dane. I don't know what makes people do anything."

"Well, I'd like to know. . . . Could you find out for me? You have to help me. I don't know what else to do."

I stared out the window. The January moon was low and white, like a ghost in the tree limbs. I thought about the bass solo he'd played with our band so many years ago. That solo—that memory—it seemed like something I needed to pay him back for.

"All right, Mr. Dane. Let's meet for lunch. Mary Mac's, one P.M. . . . What was her name, your niece?"

"Beth." I could barely hear him. "She played the flute, Mr. Tucker. Did I tell you that? She played very well. And she was studying dance."

Outside, the moon was sinking lower. I could barely see it over the windowsill. "Good night, Mr. Dane."

"Good night, Mr. Tucker."

Just as I hung up, a wood dove sitting in the tree where I'd seen the ghost of the moon called out several notes. They were silver, flutelike notes, and they hung like mist in the air even after the notes themselves were gone and the dove had flown away.

ALSO BY PHILLIP DEPOY

Easy

Too Easy

Easy as One, Two, Three

Messages from Beyond

DANCING MADE EASY

Phillip DePoy

A DELL BOOK

Published by Dell Publishing
a division of
Random House, Inc.
1540 Broadway
New York, New York 10036

This novel is a work of fiction. Names, characters, places, and incidents either are the product of the author's imagination or are used fictitiously. Any resemblance to actual persons, living or dead, events, or locales is entirely coincidental.

ISBN: 0-440-22618-X

Printed in the United States of America

Published simultaneously in Canada

November 1999

10   9   8   7   6   5   4   3   2   1

OPM

For

the late archetype of the phoenix,
the even resurgence of the kiss,
and every new birth of spirit

find four to name three

CONTENTS

DANCING
MADE EASY

1

Ill Wind at Dawn

The corpse was swaying in an angular fashion. It was moving in a little box step, hanging from the lamppost in the icy morning air. I was staring up at it.

"What exactly is that thing tied around her neck?"

"That's an apron, Flap."

Joepye Adder had lived on and off in Piedmont Park, like a phantom, since 1983. Every once in a while the constabulary would take pity on his free-wheeling ways and invite him to a nice little cell for dinner. But once he got out, he'd usually wander back to the park, and most people in the upwardly mobile neighborhoods around the park had grown to feel more uncomfortable when they *didn't* see him around.

I squinted. "An apron?"

"Come on around on this side." He pulled his coat

around him and motioned, stumbling a little from the abundance of alcohol he'd doubtless consumed before coming to my place.

I followed in his direction and got a better look. Sure enough, sticking out behind her, like a little cape, was an old-fashioned flowered apron. Wrapped around her neck, its strings were all that kept her up in the air, tied to the lamppost arm.

"Wow, Joe. Good catch."

It was just after dawn. The lamp blinked off.

"Flap, what makes the lights go on and off like that? Is it a timer, or do they have some sort of light sensor on there?"

"Joe, could we stick to one line of inquiry at a time?"

"Huh?"

"You got me up before daybreak, I'm not awake, I'm trying hard not to think about what I'm looking at. You got me down here in the cold wind, you *know* you're probably going to get me into some kind of trouble, and the issue is *not* what makes the street-lights go on and off."

He nodded. "Oh. Right. You're absolutely right, Flap. Sorry."

"You just came to get me when you saw this? You didn't call the cops?"

He twisted a little, like he was trying to get away from a bee. "What the hell'd I call a cop for?"

Despite the grisly image, I was still fascinated, in the most macabre and sleepless sense of the word, by the fact that a little cloth string was strong enough to hold up a grown woman. "You found a dead body."

"To me"—he shook his head—"if it's on the ground, like, under a pile of leaves or like that—well, that's finding a dead body. This, see, falls into a whole 'nother category—in *my* mind, at least."

"I see. So you came to me."

"I figured you to get some work out of this." He grew animated. "And then, when you got paid, I had it in mind that it'd be worth something to you to, you know, toss a little percentage my way, kind of like an agent. I mean, I know ordinarily you let Miss Dally take care of all that sort of a deal, but what her being gone to Paris and all—"

"Joe?" I gave him a little smile. "She's been back for six months."

"She has?"

"Uh-huh, and excuse me for saying so, but that says a whole lot about your sorry state."

"Sorry state?" He wasn't offended; he just questioned my choice of words. "I personally prefer to think of myself as more of your happy, carefree vagabond."

I blinked. "In what century?"

"Yeah," he had to agree. "It's a mean time in history to try for anything like 'carefree,' I can see that. Still, it's my lot in life."

"Very philosophical." I looked back up. "What's making her sway like that? Is it that windy?"

He stared skyward too. "Could be your rotation of the earth."

"No." I let my shoulders sag. "It could *not* be the rotation of the earth."

He shrugged. "Just a thought."

"You know I've got to call Dally about this."

"What for?" He made a face. "That'll just make my percentage go down."

"Because"—I raised my eyebrows—"I want to."

"Oh."

"Isn't it kind of amazing that the apron string is enough to keep her up there?"

He moved around to get another angle. "I guess." More squinting. "How old you think she was?"

"Young." I looked at her little hands. "I'm saying very early twenties."

He was looking at her clothes. "I'd wager she was a hooker."

"I guess." I shrugged.

Leather coat, tight black pants, blue ankle boots, not much of a blouse as far as I could tell from my vantage point. Could have been a wig, the hair was pretty well done up. She was wearing one of those rings, the kind you get in a bubble gum machine, plastic gold band, huge blue plastic stone.

Joepye tilted his head almost parallel to the ground. "Flap? Look. What's that on her coat?"

I took a step to where he was. I followed his gaze. "Looks like a . . . big pin. Is it a pin?"

She was pretty high up there, all things considered. Her head was only inches away from the light fixture, and the daylight was still pretty dim.

"I think," he spoke slowly, "it's a note. Look."

I did. "Maybe you've got something. Looks like it could be a note, pinned to her lapel. Man."

He looked at me. "You just plan to leave her up there, Flap, or are you going to get her down?"

"Me? Why is it my business to get her down?"

"Well"—he shook his head—"you can't just leave her up there. School kids walk this way to Grady High over there. You can't have them walking under a thing like this. It's very uncomfortable."

But before I could figure out how to get up there and do anything about it, there was a hideous rending of fabric above our heads, and the girl in question plummeted to the pavement between us like a wet sack of sand.

We stared.

Much to my shame, he was the first to gather his wits.

"Well, there you are."

I stared down at her, but not for long. She was just a kid, but it wasn't a kid's face; it was navy blue and twisted. It looked like a gargoyle, like the kind that's supposed to be a representation of the North Wind, all swollen and puffed up, tongue stuck out, blowing up a storm. If you hang by your neck long enough, you get like that. Anybody would.

The note on her lapel was written in ornate, time-consuming calligraphy. All it said was "Number One: The Tarantella."

2

JONES FOR JANEY

Well after midnight that night, with the early morning's event still less than twenty-four hours on my mind, I was in the middle of an unexpected and somewhat uncomfortable conversation at Easy.

"Go ahead." I was smiling. "Fire away. Bullets bounce off me, but if you feel like shooting off your little pistol, be my guest. Maybe you'll get something out of your system."

I admit this was, by and large, an idle boast on my part. I had never actually had the experience of bullets bouncing off any part of me. But when you have a person as angry as Mickey "The Pineapple" Nichols staring down his loaded .44 at you, well, it's my experience that you'll say almost anything. And I'd also just finished the last good bottle of wine in my reserve, so my mood was somewhat . . . expansive.

My take on this matter goes like this: If you're calm, and you claim that you can take or leave a couple of slugs, the actual threat factor can go out the window; then the person with the gun will sit down and be reasonable. Works about ten to one. These are good odds, the proof of which is that I am still here—and the exception to which is that I have several conversational scars that I occasionally show at parties.

"But as long as you're here, Mick, why don't you tell me what's on your mind."

He kept his .44 pointed directly at my head. "You are no good. This is all I am saying to you on the subject." I could smell the gin on his breath.

"I'm no good?" I jutted my head a little toward him. "What could possibly lead you to such a terrible, misguided conclusion."

"Janey."

Oh. Janey Finster. The girl Mick had often referred to as his "pride and joy." The girl who had just been found smothered to death in her own bed. The girl who had also recently taken refuge on my couch from the very person who was standing in front of me and aiming to shoot me. *Yes,* I thought then, *this may be something of a problem after all.*

"Mick." I softened my voice, partly to calm him down, partly because I was genuinely saddened at the mention of her name. "Janey is no longer with us. She is no longer anybody's pride and joy. This is a sad story. Why bring it up?"

His gun dipped a little, and his eyes unfocused for a moment. "Little Janey."

"You know," I took advantage of his lapse, "she always spoke very highly of you."

With that, his gun fell to his side. "She did? Even at the end, after our fight?"

"It's a fact." I took a step closer to him.

Easy, the club, was empty but for the two of us. The lights were low, and the clock on the wall was complaining about the fact that it was three-thirty in the morning. I had told Hal, the bartender, that I would lock up the joint, and he knew that I would take care of everything.

The only time I ever got any peace and quiet, it seemed to me, was when I was alone at Easy. My apartment house was noisy around the clock, and my life in general was a little cluttered. But ordinarily, when I was the last to lock up at the club, I had my moment of solitude. We all need a little solitude every so often. The funny thing was that I had been using that solitude, on that particular night, to mull over everything I had in my own mind about Janey Finster.

So you can imagine my dismay when, instead of same, I was interrupted by a drunken cuckold with a pistol.

Now, a cuckold is not, as Joepye had once told me, a bird that makes pleasant sounds. It is a guy that has been stiff-armed in the department d'amour. This is my definition of a cuckold, and Mickey "The Pineapple" Nichols was one such example—although that was by no means his only problem.

He had acquired his nickname, for example, not by being prickly on the outside—although he was—nor by having a wild-shock sort of hairstyle—which he did—but by being known as a guy who would, given the proper provocation, toss a hand grenade into your bed whilst you were asleep in it. People who have served their country in the armed forces will often refer to a hand grenade as a pineapple. This is my explanation of his nickname.

I moved one step closer to him. "Would you mind very much if I sat down, Mick?"

He shook his head to chase away the ghosts in it and looked at me. "Oh, jeez, by all means. Look how late it is, and here I am just going on and on about my own problems. I should let you talk. You are the one with the scintillating conversational techniques."

This was another thing to know about Mickey. He fancied himself something of a wordsmith. He would just as soon toss a ten-dollar phrase at you as he would a hand grenade.

I sat. "Yes. Scintillating."

His shoulders slumped. "Flap? I'm sorry I pointed my pistol at your head. I don't know what's come over me lately."

I shrugged. "Love makes a man do strange things. It's even in the Bible."

"Is it?"

"Or it ought to be."

He squinted his big eyes at me. "Did she really speak well of me, Flap?"

"Whenever your name came up in the conversation

around here, Mickey," I smiled, "she would say the most glowing things. How you were a gentleman—"

"And my vocabulary?"

"I was getting to that: how you had the biggest vocabulary of any man she had ever been with."

"Really?" His eyes moistened. "The biggest?"

"By far."

Finally he slumped into the seat opposite me. "Flap. What are we going to do?"

I didn't mean it to sound harsh when I said, "Janey is dead, Mick. What *can* we do?" But maybe it did sound a little rough.

Bing, he was agitated again. He moved like a firecracker. His hand flew up toward me, and the gun was no more than two inches from my nose. His face was red, and he was spitting while he talked. "What can we do? I'll tell you what we can do. We can shoot you in the head ten or twelve times and see how that makes us feel. You took her away, Flap! You took her away from me!"

"No, I did not." I tried not to move. "There was never anything between Janey and me. I barely knew her. She came to my place when she left you because she didn't want to wake up with an explosive device on her pillow and I am widely known as a sucker for a pretty face."

He wouldn't hear of it. "You took her, Flap! I'll pop you six ways from Sunday!" And the gun touched my cheek.

* * *

Now maybe if this story were being told by someone else, it would be more suspenseful, because unless it is to be a very short story, it would seem obvious that Mickey did not kill me that night. I'm saying this so we can all relax and get on with the tale without fear of some kind of bloodbath. On the other hand, what if he shot out my eye, for instance, or mutilated my face in some horrible way? So, I would still not be completely out of the woods.

"You're not mad at me, Mick. You came to me so you could get *over* being mad by talking with someone you knew would be sympathetic to your situation, which is me. I will *not* get mad back at you, because that is not my way, and you know it. You are truly mad at Foggy Moskovitz." I was guessing.

"Foggy Moskovitz." Mickey let out a growl like an animal. He jerked the gun from my face and fired it five times into the gentlemen's rest room door. So I'd made a good guess. Outside, dogs began to bark.

I let the smoke clear. Then I leaned back and folded my arms. "Feel better?"

He pressed his lips together, thought about it. "Yes."

"Are you sure?"

"What do you care?" He arched an eyebrow. "Bullets bounce off you."

"If I'm in the right mood." I nodded. "But what if I'm off my game tonight? You have a very good gun."

"The gun, yes." He glanced at the bathroom door.

"But look at my pattern. It stinks. It's all over the place."

I looked at the bullet holes in the door. It was a mess. "You're right. Maybe you're tense and squeezing too hard."

"I'm not concentrating." He set the gun down on the table between us, almost as if it had offended him. "I think that's the problem."

"You have a lot on your mind."

He intertwined his fingers together and leaned toward me. "You don't know the half of it."

"So, then," I took in a breath, "tell me."

"Well, Flap"—he closed his eyes—"just kick me in the head when I tell you, but the cops think *I'm* the one that killed Janey."

"Well, Mickey, you have to admit you can see why they might think this. You go all over town with your guns and your grenades and you punch this guy and you threaten that guy and by and by everybody in town knows what you are liable to do—plus they all know about your Jones for Janey."

"That's what's wrong with this redneck city." He clenched his teeth. "They don't understand how sensitive a guy like me can be."

Somewhere outside there were sirens joining the chorus of dogs, sirens coming our way.

"What's wrong with Atlanta, my brother, if you don't mind my saying it"—I sat up—"is an influx of guys like you."

There. I'd said it. He could shoot me or not. I grew up in Atlanta, in the shadow of the Wren's Nest, where Joel Chandler Harris stole his stories from his African servants. I made out in the balcony of the theatre that premiered *Gone with the Wind,* the theatre they tore down to put up a high-rise office building. I am the closest thing we have in my city to a native. It was guys like Mickey, with their Yankee gangster ways, who had helped to wreck the entire ambience of the city, and I didn't mind telling him so.

But he was on the sorry side of town at that point. He laid his head on the table. "You are right. I am no good. Just take my pistol and put one right in the temple. You would do me a favor."

"No," I shook my head, "I wouldn't."

"The only woman I ever loved is dead," his voice was soft, "and the cops think I am the one that killed her. What could be worse?"

I could think of a dozen things that could be worse without even trying. I could have been all shot up, for instance. That certainly would have been worse, at least in my book.

But I did my best to sympathize. "So, no kidding— why did you come to me? You know I didn't take your girl away from you. You know that is not my way, and besides, it's true that I hardly knew the girl."

"Yeah. I know that." His head stayed down. "I just . . ." He let the sentence hang.

"Well"—I straightened—"I'm going to stand up now and go get you a drink."

That got his head off the table. "Just the thing. But, Flap?"

I hesitated. "Yes?"

"After you get me that drink?"

"Yes?"

"Will you help me find out who killed Janey?"

"What?"

"Yeah. That's what I'm really here for, see?" Heavy sigh. "Help me, Flap."

In his voice I could hear the echo of the loss everybody felt now that Janey was gone. I caught myself thinking about how her hair was the color of honey, and her voice was just as sweet. I hadn't really ever spent much time with her. We'd had a few conversations over a glass or two at Easy, and she occasionally turned the house upside down with her swing dancing late nights at the club. But those few moments had made me feel she was like my kid sister. She'd had that effect on most people, I'd imagine.

Word around town was that she never had an unkind thing to say about anybody—even Mickey at his worst. She stood by him when he was drunk and never complained.

She also picked the numbers right at least twice a week, so she always had plenty of her own dough. She had a charmed life—up to a point, obviously.

I'd gotten an invitation to her memorial service. She'd always wanted, it had been said, to be cremated and planted in the Botanical Garden in Piedmont Park. So it occurred to me in that odd moment that all that was left of little Janey were the long strands of blond hair on my sofa where she'd slept the night.

"Well, since you have such a persuasive argument,

not to mention such a fine firearm," I told him, "I'd like to know who killed Janey my own self."

Just then there was a mighty bashing of wood and metal, and dozens of Atlanta's boys in blue swarmed into our little haven, guns drawn, flashlights pointing, voices mean.

"Down on the floor!"

We obliged.

There was an explosion of activity that involved questions about shots being fired. This was followed by handcuffs and all manner of loose accusations.

Within the space of nine minutes I was being examined by paramedics, even though I had explained over and over again that I had no holes in me. Mickey had told everybody loud and clear that he'd tried to shoot me. He did this, as he later told me, so that the police would not take me to jail. He wanted me out and about and looking for Janey's killer.

So a short while later Mickey "The Pineapple" Nichols was on his way to jail for the murder of little Janey Finster. I was safe and warm at Easy, dialing the phone.

3

GHOST FLUTE

"Hello?" Her voice was gravelly.

I smiled. "This is a switch, me waking you up with a phone call at four in the morning."

"Flap?"

"I'm at the club. There's been . . . an incident."

I could hear her sit up. "What?"

"Got a visit from the Pineapple."

"Mickey?" Dally's voice got hard. "Mickey was in my club? Are you all right?"

"Yeah. But you've got a bathroom door that's not going to make it."

"A what?"

"Mickey shot up the place a little."

"But you're okay." She was awake now, I could tell.

"Yeah, not a scratch on me. He's off to jail."

"It was about Janey." Her voice was even tougher.

"Bingo."

"What's the matter? You're awfully terse." Beat. "You're not alone."

"Right."

"Cops." She knew.

"They'd like to speak with you."

"Uh-huh."

I handed the phone over to an officer.

"Ms. Oglethorpe?" He spoke calmly. "There's been an incident at your establishment."

He listened.

"Yes, ma'am." His voice softened. "Everything's under control."

More listening. A smile.

"That's right. We know what to do. You can just get on down to us in the—" She'd apparently interrupted him. "That's right. The precinct house." Bigger smile. "Yes, ma'am. I know you've been there before. Everybody still talks about those little ham biscuits you brought over just this last Christmas." Nodding. "Yes. He's right here."

He handed the phone back to me. "She wants to talk to you again." One last grin. "She surely is a pistol."

I nodded. "Don't I know it."

He was off.

I waited until I thought he was out of earshot. "You could charm the color off a hard hat."

"Smooth talk for a man who's been shot up at four in the morning."

"How many people do I have to convince," I sighed, "I have *not* been shot up. I swear to God I'd know if I had a bullet in me."

"Well"—I could hear her settle back into her bed—"then why don't you go home and get some sleep? I want you to go with me to the cops tomorrow."

"I'm not pressing charges."

"Okay. I still want you to go."

"I'm not pressing charges because Mickey wants me to find out who bopped Janey."

"Oh. That's why he shot up my club?"

"He just wanted to get my attention."

"And he did."

The policemen were beginning to clear out. The one who'd spoken with Dally wandered back my direction.

"We'd like you to lock up now, Mr. Tucker, and get you on home, if you don't mind. I'll see you back to your place, if you like."

Before I could make a smart counteroffer, I heard Dally's voice in my ear. "Be nice. Let him see you home—for my sake. Get some sleep. Call me in the morning."

I nodded. "Who am I to skip the path of least resistance?"

She hung up.

I set the phone down on the bar.

The policeman stared at me. "You remember when

Ms. Oglethorpe brought us those ham biscuits Christmas Eve?"

I lifted my head. "Who do you think helped her carry them in?"

"I thought that was you." He nodded, then he looked at the floor. "You Ms. Oglethorpe's boyfriend?"

"Me? Naw."

Still not looking at me. "What are you then?"

"I," big old heavy breath, "am too tired to explain it."

He took a second, then he looked up at me. "Well, be good to her, hear? She's the closest thing we've got to an angel—at least on this street."

I looked at him good for the first time. He was only a kid, maybe not that long out of high school. Maybe he was far away from home. Maybe he still wasn't used to gunshots at 4:00 A.M., and hookers slicing each other up over five dollars, and guys with five-dollar nicknames who killed people with hand grenades. Maybe Dally's ham biscuits were the closest thing to home he'd had in a while.

"I'd say amen to that."

He seemed to be satisfied with my answer. We shoved off. He followed me as I drove the short distance home and waved when I went in. I was in bed by four-thirty.

Now, ordinarily that would have been the end of a relatively average day for yours truly, but just as I was nodding off, the phone rang again.

I grabbed at it. "Who's calling me at this time of night?"

There was a pause on the other end of the line. "I tried calling earlier, but there was no answer."

"You still haven't answered my question."

"Is this Mr. Tucker? Flap Tucker?"

I opened my eyes. "Don't make me ask for the third time."

"It's Irgo Dane, here."

"Irgo Dane?" That made me sit up. "The bass player?"

"Do you know me?" He sounded genuinely surprised.

"I've heard you play."

Irgo Winfred Dane was, in my humble opinion, the finest bass player in the South. Played with the Atlanta Symphony Orchestra, the Opera Orchestra, and also alongside the finest jazz singers in town. He could flat play anything. He was known around town as something of an oddball, but for his kind of genius you make allowances, in my book.

I managed to get myself up on one elbow. "You sat in once with my band—a long time ago, back in the old days." He'd played "Big Noise from Winnetka."

"I did?" He sounded almost shy about it. "Please forgive me, I play with so many people. . . ."

"Don't apologize." I cleared my throat. "God. I wouldn't expect you to remember. But it was a big night for me."

"How very kind of you to say so."

"So you're calling me?"

"Oh. Yes, I am. You . . . now I've got you on the phone, I don't quite know what to say."

"Start with the topic of the call."

"Well. That would be my niece."

"What about her?"

"Well, you found her body this morning, I believe."

Stop the presses. "That girl hanging from the lamppost by the park this morning was your *niece*? Are you sure?"

"Fairly certain. I've been with the police all day." A moment of silence. "I could barely stand to look at her face, I doubt I could have told anything from that mess . . . they used her fingerprints to identify the body. I'm afraid I wasn't really much help at all."

"I see. Well." Trying to clear my head. "How would you know I had anything to do with finding her? I left before the police got there." Joe had found the body. Let him stay with it until the police came, that had been my thinking.

"You *do* know a Mr. Adder."

"Yes, I do."

"He was the one—"

"Wait." I had to stop him. "How would *you* know him?"

"Well," he was beginning to sound very tired. "I live close to the park, and on occasion I've found Mr. Adder in my gazebo. When it rains, mostly. I give him coffee, and he sometimes does a little yard work for me, you know. He needs the money, you see."

"And so Joepye told you that I found your niece?"

"Well, actually he said he'd found her, then contacted you. He said you were the man to help me."

I rubbed my face. "What kind of help were you looking for exactly? This is a police case."

"They only think of my niece as another dirty street person." Sigh. "But she was just a little girl. I was just remembering, as a matter of fact"—his voice was getting hoarse—"about her third birthday. I gave her a Raggedy Ann doll, an antique. It was quite expensive, even then. She didn't know, of course. She sleeps with it to this day. She told me on the phone only last month when we talked at Christmas." Silence. "It's very difficult for me to think of that same girl as . . . what the police think she was."

"They probably think she was a prostitute."

If I'd been less tired, that wouldn't have come out so rough. But he took it well enough.

"She probably was." His voice was thick. "But she wanted to get out of that life."

"She did?" I wondered if they'd been close enough to discuss any of that.

"I'd assume so, wouldn't you? She was just a little girl."

"Yeah." I let out my breath. "She was kind of like a little girl, I guess."

"What would make a person do something like that, something so horrible, to a little girl?"

"I don't know, Mr. Dane. I don't know what makes people do anything."

"Well, I'd like to know." His voice was weaker,

but also somehow weirder. I didn't think much of it—
at the time. "Could you find out for me?"

"What?"

His voice got stronger again. "The police might
find out who killed her. I mean, if they don't, I'd like
you to help with that too. But I want you to find out
why this happened. I want to understand it better. I
want to understand what that note meant, the note
pinned to her body."

"Look, Mr. Dane"—I shifted in bed—"usually,
there aren't the kind of clear answers like you're looking for. The person who did this, they're probably just
nuts. There's no real rhyme or reason to a murder like
this. I mean, the police . . ."

"You have to help me. I don't know what else to
do."

I stared out the window. The January moon was
low and white, like a ghost in the tree limbs. I thought
about that bass solo he'd played with our band so
many years ago. That solo—that memory—it seemed
like something I needed to pay him back for.

"All right, Mr. Dane. Let's meet for lunch. Mary
Mac's, one P.M."

"Yes." Big sigh on the other end of the line.
"Good. Thank you, Mr. Tucker."

"What was her name, your niece?"

"Hepzibah. She was named after the sister of
Yehudi Menuhin."

"Hepzibah? What did you call her?"

"Beth." I could barely hear him. "Most people
called her Beth. She played the flute, Mr. Tucker. Did I

tell you that? She played very well. And she was studying dance."

"I'm sorry for your loss, Mr. Dane."

"This is everyone's loss, Mr. Tucker. My niece is
dead, and a lifetime of people will never get to know
what a wonderful child she was—so beautiful, such
talent, so very bright."

Outside, the moon was sinking lower. I could
barely see it over the windowsill.

"Good night, Mr. Dane."

"Good night, Mr. Tucker."

Just as I hung up, a wood dove sitting in the tree
where I'd seen the ghost of the moon called out several
notes. They were silver, flutelike notes, and they hung
like mist in the air even after the notes themselves
were gone and the dove had flown away.

4

REMEMBRANCE OF
THINGS PAST

I was up by eleven the next morning, but not because I
wanted to be.

I picked up the offending appliance and stared at
it, but that didn't make any difference. The thing just
kept on ringing.

So I finally answered. "I'm thinking of having this
phone disconnected."

"Wouldn't help." Dally's voice was wide-awake.
"I'd just come over and bang on your door."

"I suppose."

"Beautiful morning outside. Unfortunately I'm inside staring at a bathroom door that's definitely shot
to hell."

I tried to sit up. "I told you."

"You sound a little sleepy there, pal."

"Yeah. When I got home last night? I got another call."

"A phone call?"

"Irgo Dane."

"The bass player?" Her voice softened. "You're kidding."

"Himself. And you'll never guess why he was calling."

"At four-thirty in the morning."

"Right." I nodded. "Perhaps you'll recall my little adventure with Joepye yesterday morning?"

"The kid hanging in the park." Softer still. "Hard to forget that image."

"Tell me. Anyway, the kid? She was Dane's niece."

"No."

"That's what he said."

She sounded like she was sitting down. "And why would he lie about a thing like that?"

"Right. I'm meeting him at Mary Mac's for lunch. Care to join us?"

"What time?" She hadn't paused for even a breath.

"One."

"Okay." She was moving again, I could tell. "One it is. We can go to the police station after that."

"Dally?"

"Hmm?"

"He wants to hire me to find out why somebody did that to his niece. Dane does."

"Well, that figures." She laughed. "So that makes Mickey shooting up my place to get you to find out who killed little Janey, and Dane calling you in the wee hours to ask you to find out about his niece. You certainly lead an interesting life these days."

"See you at lunch."

Only a three-block walk down Ponce de Leon from the Fabulous Fox, Mary Mac's Tea Room may be the last one of its kind left in the country. Packed at lunchtime every day, it conveys many of the best things about a South that's mostly gone.

I don't mean gone with the wind either. It took more than a breeze to take out my city. It took Sherman burning it to the ground and a horde of invading infidels salting the earth for the next one hundred years. It took an army of Sherman's grandson-businessmen turning my city into a second-rate convention center and a first-rate example of downtown decay. The symbol of the city may be the phoenix, but its emblem could just as well be the weasel. Not that I'm against business—in its place. I just lament the way business does business around here.

Still, Mary Mac's was packed with businessmen when I got there a little before one, so you'd at least have to say they knew where to eat. The noise of the crowd was as soothing to me as the sound of ocean waves.

I had just gotten my heavy overcoat off when the hostess raised her eyebrows at me. "Hey there, Flap. You all by yourself today?"

"Naw." I shook my head. "Dally's coming. And we have a guest."

She nodded. "By the window?"

I headed for the table. "Absolutely."

I sat and stared out the window. I watched the traffic go by, hoping to get some of the pictures from the previous night's sleep out of my head. Try as I might, the image of that body swinging in the chilly air kept alternating with the sleeping face of Janey Finster in my mind.

I didn't even notice that Dally had come in. Which was an indication of how far away from normal I actually was.

"Flap?"

"Oh. Hey."

"Jeez, what's on your mind?" She sat beside me. The very faint perfume was like hyacinths.

"My mind?"

"The way you're staring out that window." She shook her head. "Maybe you're not awake yet."

"Not entirely. How's the club? Any other damage besides the door?"

"No. But next time you're there all by yourself? Lock up *before* the men with guns get there, okay?"

"Men with Guns, I loved their first album."

"So"—she put her napkin in her lap—"what makes Dane think the kid on the lamppost was his niece?"

"He's the one they called to identify the body. You know how they like to have some unhappy family member look at the body to make it official."

"What about fingerprints?"

I nodded. "That's what they had to use. No ID on

her, and that face was pretty messy. I don't see how anybody could have identified that."

"She'd been beaten?"

"No, but the . . . you really want to talk about this before lunch?"

She shrugged. "Just don't get too graphic."

"Sometimes"—I tilted my head to one side—"the face can get a little gargoylelike in a hanging body situation, is all."

Timing being everything, Irgo Winfred Dane chose that moment to enter the establishment.

I stood.

He turned heads. He was a big man, entirely bald, regal, hard to miss, and lots of people had seen him play, or seen his likeness in the papers, mostly the Sunday arts section.

"Mr. Dane."

He took my hand and squeezed very firmly. "Mr. Tucker." He looked down. "And you must be Ms. Oglethorpe."

"Yes, I suppose I must be." She stood too.

"I thought so." He took her hand.

"See?" I smiled at her. "Your reputation precedes you."

They shook hands.

He sat at our little round table, across from Dally and beside me, leaving the fourth chair, directly by the window, vacant so we could all see out at the pansies in the window box.

He picked up a little stub pencil and an order ticket. "I'm very hungry."

Dally smiled, and started filling in her ticket too.

All I wanted was the vegetable plate—but not for health reasons. I got fried okra, fried squash, turnip greens boiled with ham, and black-eyed peas boiled in other ham. Might as well have been a fatty hamburger, but I knew that it surely would eat good.

Once the waitress had picked up our tabs, we got down to business.

"Mr. Dane, do you have any idea how the cops got to you so quickly in the first place? There was very little in the way of identification or clues as to who that young woman was, as far as I could tell, and random fingerprint searches usually take more than a few hours."

Dane looked surprised. "Didn't your friend tell you?"

I glanced over at Dally. "My friend?"

"Mr. Adder."

"Tell me what?"

He leaned back. "He knew her. He knew Beth."

I looked at Dally again. "Her name was Hepzibah, but everyone called her Beth."

Dally kept her eye on Dane. "I'm glad for her sake. What's this about Joepye knowing her?"

He let go a hefty sigh and closed his eyes for a moment. "He'd seen her in the park . . . working. He recognized her clothes."

I nodded. "They were fairly distinctive."

He agreed. "Yes."

"But Joepye knew who she was," Dally pushed, "and didn't tell Flap?"

Dane squinted. "Yes. That comes as a surprise to me too."

I leaned forward. "And once they knew who she was, why didn't the cops call her parents?"

Dane looked at the tabletop. "They wouldn't have come. They'd given up on her. They didn't even care enough to take care of her arrangements. I've had to see to her cremation." He shook his head. "And they live in Hilton Head now anyway. I was the nearest relative."

I sat back. "And the police knew who she was because of Joepye, who got me out of bed early in the morning to stare at the body but didn't tell me *he* knew who she was."

Dane's voice was hesitant. "Excuse me, I know Mr. Adder is a friend of yours, but wouldn't you describe him as a little . . . confused most of the time?"

"Oh, he's confused all right," I nodded, "but he's usually consistently confused. I'm just saying he had the presence of mind to think of the situation as a case, but he held back some fairly key information. Why did he do that?"

Silence.

Dally arranged her silverware. "We kind of skipped the part where we were supposed to tell you we were sorry about your niece's being . . . gone."

Dane lifted his head.

I nodded. "Sorry."

He looked out the window. "How does it happen that a beautiful child—and so intelligent—loses her way so deeply? What makes that happen?"

I looked down. "I know that's what you want, Mr. Dane. You want me to find out why her life went the way it did and why these things happened to her. Finding the murderer is almost secondary to you."

He nodded, still staring out at the street. "I don't want revenge or even justice, in that sense. I just want an explanation."

I knew what he meant. It's tough to figure why we're all so cold sometimes, when all we want is a little kindness and a chance to be happy at the end of the day. After all, every dead hooker was somebody's little girl. Still, it occurred to me then to wonder why we weren't at least mentioning the odd note about the tarantella that had been pinned to the body. He had talked about it last night. But maybe Mr. Dane just wasn't as interested in dancing as he said Beth had been.

In fact he seemed to be completely lost for a second or two. Then he looked back at us. "I don't want to suspect Mr. Adder."

Just like that.

Dally nodded. "So why would you?"

He looked at me. "Don't you find his lack of disclosure disturbing?"

"I do," I assured him. "But I'd be a long way from suspecting Joepye of anything at all. He's a harmless old guy. Back in the days when he was teaching at Tech . . ."

But I couldn't finish. Dane's eyes widened. "That man taught at *Georgia Tech*?"

"Yeah." I resumed. "Electrical engineering. He hasn't always been a drunk, you know."

"But"—Dane sat back—"electrical engineering?"

I couldn't quite figure out why he seemed so shocked. "Okay, so it was mostly courses about wiring houses for building contractors. He was pretty good at it, though."

"What happened to him?"

I leaned forward. "You don't sit in your grammar school and say to yourself, 'When I grow up, I'm going to fall in love with alcohol and not be able to stop.' You're not born a lush."

"No," he nodded slowly, "I guess you're not."

"I started to say that when he was at Tech, he had the reputation of being able to keep a secret and not gossip—apparently something of a unique quality in the academic world. He's just a little closemouthed, is all. He doesn't smear his smarts all over the place."

Dane was still staring out into space. "No, he certainly doesn't. In fact you'd hardly know at all." Little sigh. "I'll let my suspicions relax—for the time being."

"Good."

"It's just that his connection with this situation seems a little coincidental."

Dally looked down at her place mat. "Uh-oh."

Dane cocked his head in her direction.

I filled him in. "She's making mock of my predilection for dismissing coincidence."

"Dismissing it?"

"I think there's no such thing. It always means something. It's never really just random, accidental events that only *seem* to have been planned or arranged. Somehow, they actually *were* planned or arranged."

Dally touched my arm but looked at Dane. "Let him eat, Mr. Dane. He's much more coherent after he's eaten."

Once again timing interceded, and our food arrived. We ate it with very little conversation.

When the plates were empty, Dane dabbed his mouth and threw the napkin on the table in front of him. "So, will you do this for me, Mr. Tucker? Will you find out why this happened?"

I sipped my sweet tea. "Have you got a recent photo? I don't even know what she looked like, really. Sorry to say this, but you realize yesterday's look at her doesn't count."

"Yes, I thought you might need one." He fished in his wallet for a moment. "This was just taken at Christmas. Will it do?" It was a sweet face, smiling, holding up an unopened package, a strangely familiar face. But it couldn't really have been familiar to me, given that grim blue mask she'd worn the only time I'd ever seen her.

I breathed in. "What if the answer's only that sometimes these kids get killed for no reason?"

"I'll still want details."

I wadded up my napkin. "What if the cops find out about all that first?"

He squinted. "They won't. Not the way I want."

"Why not?"

He folded his arms in front of him. "Mr. Tucker,

don't you have a person you care very much about in this world? And if you do, wouldn't you want to know more than the *facts* if something like this happened? Wouldn't you want an investigation of this sort to be more . . . personal?"

I nodded slowly. "I guess I would." And there it was again: the sleeping profile of little sister Janey floating in my mind. "You want me to do this because the cops take it as business, and you know I'll take it personally."

"That's your reputation."

"According to Joepye Adder."

He flexed his forehead. "According to the police, actually."

"You asked them about me?"

"I did."

"And they told you I would take it personally?"

Dally smiled. "Your reputation precedes you."

Dane reached into his suit coat. "Shall I make out a check now to retain you? Is that customary?"

I rubbed my right eye. "Mind if I talk it over with Ms. Oglethorpe for a while? We've got to go to the police station now on some other business, and I rarely do anything at all without talking to her first."

He nodded. "I understand." He shifted and went for his wallet. "Here's my card. Call me." He also pulled out his credit card. "Lunch is on me."

Dally smiled. "Thank you, Mr. Dane. That's very kind."

I turned to face him. "One night, I don't know exactly when—I guess last year sometime—I saw you play the Atlanta Opera's *Faust* over at the Fox. And that same night, much later, I saw you at that place over in Little Five Points. I saw you sit in with Mose Allison."

He smiled for the first time in our meeting. "Mose."

"You took a break on 'Was' that went all the way out of the known galaxies."

He nodded, still smiling. "Three-quarter time. Used a lot of bow. I remember."

I smiled back at him. "If I do this job for you, *that's* why. Because of that solo—and others like it."

His head flinched just like he'd been stuck with a pin, and his eyes blinked just a little too much, I thought. He sat for a moment, trying to figure out what to say to that. All he came up with was "Well."

My lips thinned. "So I'll be in touch."

I stood; Dally did likewise.

He looked up at me, then. " 'Big Noise from Winnetka.' "

It caught me off guard. "Hmm?"

He smiled. "That's what I played when I sat in with your band all those years ago. I've been trying to think of it since we talked last night."

I shook my head. "Jesus, man. How would you remember that?"

He stood too, all our checks in his hand. "You don't forget a night like that."

"I don't." I nodded. "But I figured you'd have had hundreds of nights like that."

"I have. I don't forget any of them."

He headed for the cash register.

I was right behind him. "Well, you've got a great memory."

His voice was quiet. "I do. But that's not always a good thing."

Right. For example, it suddenly occurred to me that somewhere in the city there was probably an antique Raggedy Ann doll worth a lot of money just sitting around with nobody to come home to it. I couldn't say why that had come to me exactly. But I didn't care much for the image. Something about it made me picture the face of Dane's niece, sleeping with that doll. Then, with very little effort on my part, that face was superimposed on Janey's face as she slept on my sofa. They were nearly the same. Maybe it was just because they were both kids who didn't deserve to be dead. Or maybe it was because I was having one of my moments. Sometimes it's hard to tell the difference between satori, a flashback, and cognitive dysfunction. That's one of those things that keeps a guy like me on his toes.

Nevertheless, there they were: those two sweet faces swimming in the fluid of my sight, sleeping the peace that passeth understanding—and still whispering my name.

5

FOGGY NEW YEAR

"Suicide?" I stared at the detective.

He nodded, but he didn't look me in the eye.

Dally shook her head, staring at the floor. "She shimmied up the lamp, tied an apron string around her neck—"

I interrupted. "Don't leave out the note."

She nodded. "After pinning the mysterious note to herself, then flung herself swinging and dangled there . . ."

The detective had had enough. He closed up his notepad. "Until she expired. Yes."

I blinked. I enunciated. "And just who, do you think, will believe this?"

He finally looked at me. "It was a cry for attention."

I didn't mean to laugh at such an absurd suggestion, but it was necessary. It just made the detective mad.

"Look, Tucker, I don't see how it's any of your business anyway."

Dally smiled. Have I waxed poetical, before, about the effect of that? "Actually, Detective, Mr. Tucker has been hired by the uncle of the deceased."

Her expression had its fabled effect once more: The detective smiled back. "Yes, ma'am."

I lowered my voice. "You don't believe this suicide idea."

He looked out across the desks in the room. "I don't have to believe anything about it. That is what the facts support. There were no fingerprints anywhere on the body, the lamp, the apron, the note, or the pin. Nothing."

Dally nodded. "Not even hers?"

He still stared. "There were a few of her prints on some of her clothes."

I folded my hands in front of me. "On her shirt, inside the jacket, that sort of thing."

He gave a single nod.

I went on. "Where a person who was wiping prints away might not get to."

Another nod.

Dally leaned in. "So the thought that prints might have been wiped has occurred to you."

He was clearly irritated. "Yes, ma'am, it has. I've been investigating crime scenes for seven or eight years now. It would surely occur to me that prints might have been wiped."

I opened my hands. "Then . . ."

He stood up. "Look, we have seventeen unsolved murders pending in this precinct right at the moment, and the sad and sorry fact is that an unhappy hooker is a low priority." He finally looked at us again. "These kids, they have a high rate of suicide. A lot of them, they're very dramatic about it. You'd be surprised how much bad poetry there is in my files."

Before I could stop: "And what would qualify as good poetry to you, Detective?"

He fired right back. "I'm a Wallace Stevens fan personally. Went through a Richard Brautigan phase when I was younger, but who didn't?"

I sat back, duly chastised. I glanced at the nameplate on the desk. Detective Burnish Huyne. I nodded. He was a tough, wiry sort of guy with jet black hair falling onto his forehead and coal black eyes staring my way. "Detective Huyne."

He still sounded a little defensive. "Yes?"

"Do you have an opinion of wine?"

"What?"

Dally tried not to show her amusement.

I lifted my head in his direction. "I say, do you care about wine one way or the other?"

His eyes narrowed. "Depends."

"On?"

One shoulder lifted. "The region mostly, the year, sometimes the château."

Dally beat me to the punch line. "Louis, this looks like the beginning of a beautiful friendship."

He looked at her. "Louis?"

She brushed past the reference. "Doesn't matter. Mr. Tucker here would like to buy you a glass of something when you get off work tonight. You know where Easy is?"

He finally relaxed enough to sit back. "I heard you had a little trouble over there last night."

She nodded. "A little. That's actually why we're here today. Had to take care of the paperwork. No big deal."

I picked up. "Our visit to you was secondary. But the offer of a glass or two over at Easy still stands. I wouldn't mind discussing all this in somewhat less . . . austere surroundings."

He took a good twenty or thirty seconds of silence. Then: "I get off at seven-thirty tonight."

I smiled. "I think something in a nice St. Émilion—around '86. I'm partial to the Simard, but mostly because it's handy."

"Handy?" He blinked. "At Easy? No offense."

Dally stood. "Flap's got his own stash. See you tonight?"

He stood too. "Is there a band?"

"Gwen Hughes."

He nodded. "Jazz and cocktails."

I was the last to stand. "Lush Life."

He stuck out his hand. "I guess it's possible we could have a thing or two in common."

"By the way," I tried to make it sound like an

afterthought, "what do you make of the note you found on the kid?"

"The tarantella? It's some kind of dance, they tell me."

"Right," I smiled, "but what does *that* mean? Kind of an unusual suicide note, isn't it?"

"Not only that." He didn't bat an eye. "It's written on old-style computer printout paper, the kind that used to have holes all along the sides and then you'd tear off the holes?"

"So," I smiled politely, "it *is* an unusual suicide note, you're saying."

"I'm saying I'll see you tonight."

Huyne and I shook hands on it. I walked Dally to the door. She was headed over to the club.

"So what do you *really* think about that note?" Her voice was low.

"Well, I'll tell you. At the moment I think that somebody wants all and sundry to think it's what you'd call a clue."

"What?" She stopped for a second.

"That's right," I told her. "It's too . . . dramatic to be anything but a deliberate lead—or a *mislead*."

"Did seem a little much." She agreed, but she could see my mind was somewhere else. "Give you a lift?"

"No." I took a step back inside the station house. "I've got another stop to make here."

Wasn't the easiest thing in the world to get to talk to Mickey Nichols, but I've got my ways, including some ex-service buddies on the force, especially one Internal Affairs detective, a guy named Winston, who just happened to have had a hand in saving my life once—but I digress. Suffice it to say that twenty minutes after I'd said good-bye to Dally I was in a holding cell with the man who'd thought about killing me only the night before.

"Mick, say again what you told the cops about trying to kill me?"

He tilted his head at me. "Like I said last night, I admitted that you were an innocent bystander and that the gunplay was from when I had tried to pop you, so they would not haul you in *with* me—"

"So I could look into—"

"'Look into,' *hell,* Flap." His eyes flashed. "You've got to find out who killed Janey. I mean it."

"Easy, Mick. I'll do it."

He folded his arms. "You are known far and wide as a guy who has no belief in the notion of coincidence."

"Correct." Why was he bringing that up?

"Coincidence is for saps, as everyone knows. How far would I get thinking, for example, that Frankie Bottles had just happened to show up at a particular time in a particular place exactly when I also did?"

He was referring to Frankie "Bottles" Ording, whose primary income seemed to come from cases of liquor he'd "bought," "found," or even—my favorite—"inherited." He and Mickey had been rivals for Janey's affection in the younger days, and Frank would often show up at parties where the happy couple were just to irritate Mickey. Brawls would often ensue.

He pointed to the palm of his right hand. There was a stigmata-like scar.

"This is where Frankie tried to put an ice pick in my temple. As luck would have it, Janey saw him coming, let out a holler, and I reflexed my hand in this manner." He demonstrated the move that had saved his life. "But as you can see, I still carry a reminder of the evening's festivities." He pointed again at the scar, then wagged the same finger at me. "No. Do not try and tell me he just *happened* to be there. He came to put a sharp object into my brains, my friend."

I folded my arms. "As you were saying, you're preaching to the choir. I myself am not that big a believer in coincidence."

He wrinkled his brow. "It would not explain, for example, how it is that you get asked by me to find out who took Janey out on *exactly* the same night as you are called up by a famous bass player to look into the very strange murder of his niece."

So that's where he was going.

"You're not suggesting," I asked him, "that the two murders are related?"

"I'm not?"

I shrugged. "And, by the way, how do you know so much about this, being stuck, as you are, in jail?"

He smiled. "I've got ways."

I shook my head. "Okay, but see, it would be too much of a coincidence if the two things *did* have something in common."

"Have you seen a picture of what Dane's niece looked like before she got dead?"

I nodded. "He gave me a photo."

"Do they favor, this niece and my Janey?"

"Oh." I stared off. "That's why Dane's niece looked familiar. They *did* look alike—like cousins maybe." I had just realized it in that second. "What are you getting at?"

"Didn't I just say I've got my ways? One of my ways is intuition." But I could tell there was more to it than that.

I sighed. "All right. Let's just get a few facts before you launch off into your intuition."

"Fair enough. For instance?"

"When did you last see Janey alive?"

"New Year's Eve party at Foggy's."

Foggy Moskovitz. Even though his given name was Schlomo, no one ever called him that—mostly because he was, perhaps, the finest booster in the Atlanta metropolitan area. His specialty was cars, but he often claimed he could steal the shine off a policeman's badge if the situation called for it. He went to temple every Saturday and claimed to keep a kosher home, although I'm not certain what kind of kosher home it is that's filled with mostly stolen items.

"Foggy Moskovitz invited you to his New Year's Eve party?"

He opened his hands. "What *invited*? We just went. Everybody was there." He closed his eyes. "What a mistake that was."

"Mistake?"

"You know Foggy. He would stare at Janey while she was swing dancing—you know how she could cut a rug. Anyway, that night he started into flirting with Janey, asking her to dance with him, the way he sometimes did. And then, on top of that, I maybe had one too many of the Hot Tom and Jerry—which is an excellent New Year's Eve drink, by the way—and I get irritated, and maybe I mouth off a little."

"A little?"

"I call Foggy a thief."

I blinked. "Excuse me for mentioning it, but technically, Foggy *is* a thief."

"It was the way I said it."

"I see."

He shook his head. "Then Janey, you know, gets real mad and calls me a dope, which I am not, and I try to explain that to her, and all she can seem to do is ask Foggy is he okay."

"Which only made you worse."

He inclined his head. "Unfortunately. I would have to say that I took a pop at Foggy."

"Did you clip him?"

His voice got duller. "That's the worst part. He ducks, and I catch Janey instead. I mean, she was standing so close to him, I could hardly miss. Boy, she let me have it then. She left almost immediately—with Foggy, who was, by the way, tossing no small amount of insult my way as he egressed."

"*Egressed*. I see." I knew there was more. "Go on."

He hesitated. "And so I may have threatened to

zotz the both of them while they slept. But you know me. I'm liable to say just such a thing in the heat of the moment which I would never do in the cold light of day."

I leaned toward him. "But you can see that it's just this sort of thing that would make the police think you had something to do with the murder."

His eyes grew cold very quickly. "Lucky for me that you don't share this view."

I stared for a moment. I knew it was a question.

"Well, Mick, I know you loved Janey. You had your little fights, but nearly everybody does."

And then the cold look left his eyes, and he stared at the floor. "Why did I ever fight with her, Flap? What's the matter with me?"

"Didn't I just say nearly everybody has these little tiffs?"

He looked up at me. "Not you and Dally."

"What makes you think that?"

"Again, it is widely known."

"Yeah." I smiled, but not entirely at him. "Well, Dally and I are the exception to nearly every rule I know about."

He shrugged a little. "Yeah. I guess I can see that." He looked me in the eye. "So when are you two kids going to get together, anyway?"

"We *are* together."

He shook his head. "No. I mean in the *together* sense."

"Oh. Well." I stood. "The day after that's any of your business, I may drop you a line."

He held up his hands. "Okay. I can leave it alone."

I was about to call the turnkey when it occurred to me to show the Polaroid of Beth Dane to Mick. I slipped it out of my coat pocket.

"This is a photo of Beth Dane, by the way."

"Jesus, will you look at that kisser?" He stared. "I guess she *could* have been Janey's cousin. Like you said."

"Yeah." I nodded.

"At least"—he stared harder—"that's what I thought when I . . . Flap? Now, I can't be positive, of course . . ."

"Positive about what?"

He shook his head. "But I think I even remember commenting on it that night."

"What night?"

He squinted, thinking hard. "I *thought* so." He looked up at me. "This kid was at Foggy's party too. I *thought* I saw her there." He sat back. "So it wasn't just intuition. I saw her before."

"At the Foggy Moskovitz New Year's Eve party?"

He looked back down at the picture. "I'm pretty sure. I remember thinking how odd it was that she would be there—babe-o-liscious as she was and looking so much like Janey—in the company of that park ghost."

"Park ghost?"

He handed me back the snapshot. "You know, your pal. That little goofball Joepye what's-his-name."

6

SPIDER RHYTHM

All I really knew about Janey Finster's life away from Easy—and the dance floor—was what I'd heard from other people, mostly about her charmed life. What I knew for myself was her sweet temperament and the things she'd told me in those late-night confabulations at the club. Mostly she talked and I listened. She was just a kid, and had a kid's sense of telling an older guy like me a thing or two she'd discovered about life.

"Take it from me, men are a strange lot." She'd toss back her Jägermeister and then slap her little hand down on the bar.

I would nod, sagely. "Yes, they are. Men are, generally speaking for a person such as yourself, no good."

She'd grin and put her hand on my arm. "Ah, Flap. If it wasn't for Dally, I'd ask you out so fast."

At this I would lean back. "No. You would not. I am nearly old enough to be your father, and that's what you like about me: I'm safe."

This would hand her a laugh. "You're not close to that old—and you're about as safe as a blasting cap."

I would smile then. "You make me very happy. Now go home."

And she would.

There were probably lots of guys who would have taken advantage of a situation of that sort. I just wasn't one of them. I thought of her as a little sister. Nothing noble about it, I just knew what was what. The *real* thing in this life is primarily what they call the marriage of true minds. True minds are minds that are alike. Here's the moral: To get a great thing going, you each have to have a good mind to do it.

Case in point: "Flap. What're you doing? Thinking about Janey?"

I looked up at Dally. "How'n the world would you know that?"

She smiled. "I read you like a book."

See?

I looked at my wineglass. "Yes, you do."

"What about Janey?"

"I need to know a little more about her actual background."

She brought the rest of the less expensive Côtes du Rhône—signaling how low my backroom stash was, incidentally—and poured. I'd come directly to Easy from my visit with Mickey.

"Didn't she crash with you just before she got it?" Dally asked.

"Yeah, but we didn't talk about stuff like that."

Dally set the bottle down. "You seem to have sunk to a pedestrian grape."

I shrugged. "It'll do. And I'm a little short on cash."

"You still haven't taken Dane's check?"

I shook my head. "Haven't decided what to do about that exactly. It's already getting a little confusing."

"How?"

"For instance, I showed the snapshot of Beth Dane to the Pineapple? He said he thought he remembered seeing her at Foggy's on New Year's Eve. He also commented on her resemblance to Janey."

Dally leaned on the bar. The place was mostly empty. I guess it was around two in the morning. "Right. What did you talk about?"

"Who? Me and the Pineapple?"

"No, I mean you and Janey—when she was at your pad. You said you didn't talk about her *background* or whatever."

"Oh. Well. Mostly her troubles with Mickey, how she had a crush on Foggy Moskovitz, which I told her was just because he treated her nice and the grass is always greener and once she hooked up with him it might be the same as Mickey—that sort of thing."

She looked at me sideways. "So maybe that's the place to start—sans your advice to the lovelorn."

I sipped. "Oh, I know a thing or two about l'amour."

"Uh-huh."

"Or anyway, I know what guys like that are like."

She shook her head. "No, you don't. You've got about as much in common with Foggy and the Pineapple as I do."

"Is that right?"

"Yes, that's right." And with no warning, she leaned over and popped my cheekbone with her lips. "Thank God." Then she was off, down to the other end of the bar.

"From this," I called after her, "I determine that it is easier to understand a young girl than it is know a real live woman."

She didn't look back. "And don't you forget it."

Well, there is probably no circumstance in this old wide world where Dalliance Oglethorpe couldn't make me smile.

Even last call. I finished my glass and put the pressure stopper back in the bottle. The two weeknight barmaids began to tally out. Dally was busy at the register. I was the only customer left in the place, which was filled with the satisfying undertones that come after the final chord of the song. The light was warm, like candlelight.

I stared down at the snapshot on the bar. I was trying to get it straight in my mind just how much these two kids actually looked alike. I knew that their faces had collided in my mind, but I figured it was just because they were both dead—and I didn't even blink at the morbidity of that thought.

I did blink at the visitor, though; also smiled. "Detective Huyne. This is something of a surprise—at this time of night. I expected you more around the seven o'clock hour."

He looked over at Dally. "Too late for a final dram?"

She didn't even look up. I suppose she'd seen him come in. "Dram?"

He slumped a little. "Imagine how tough it might be to live up to a name like Burnish. You have to use words like that."

She turned to him and smiled. "And how do we choose our words if we have a name like Dalliance?"

He smiled right back. "Beautifully, in my book."

She brought a glass. I poured us both out what was left of the Côtes du Rhône.

He nodded at the bottle. "It's French and red."

I sipped. "Next time it'll be this nice little St. Émilion that I like."

Shrug. "Okay."

I set my glass down. "So, should I ask why you're so late, or should I ask why you're here at all?"

"I'm late because of work. I'm here because of you all."

I raised my eyebrows. "I'm flattered."

"Skip that. I just didn't enjoy telling a person like you that the kid up the lamppost was a suicide."

I folded my arms. "I didn't care much for that myself."

He sipped. "But that's her file. That's the story."

"You know better."

"Wouldn't anybody?"

I nodded.

He met my eyes straight. "Like I said, there're plenty of dead hookers to go around, and usually nobody comes around asking any questions, and the sorry fact is, they get written off. That's just life in the big city." He set the glass down. "But I suppose you'll be happy to know that this particular case has been opened back up."

I nodded. "Thanks to Dane."

"Exactly." He absently turned his glass. "He knows a lawyer."

"I'd imagine."

"So," his voice was hesitant, "we're doing all kinds of tests and whatnot."

"I see." I could tell he wanted to ask me something.

"So, I just thought you ought to know."

I opened my hand. "Now I know."

"If you don't tell me . . ." He stared straight ahead, and went on. "I could look it up, you know."

I shifted in my head. "Look what up?"

"The tarantella."

"Oh." I smiled. "Well. I guess you could look that up."

He sighed. "But you already know what it is, don't you?"

"Yes." I took in a breath. "I guess I do."

"Okay, look." He finished his glass. "I know what your rep is. I admire it in an odd way. It's not police work, but you seem to get the job done most of the time. And I like the company." He stared up at Dally.

I looked at Dally too, and I had to ask her then, "Since when did you come to be known as the policeman's friend?"

She shot me a look. "The what?"

"Ham biscuits at Christmas." I smiled back. "Detective Huyne here, making with the compliments all of a sudden—"

"You can't run a place like this," her voice was light, "at least not on Ponce, without becoming chummy with all sorts of people. How many times do you think the cops have kept this place from being messed up?"

I shrugged. "On average? Ten times a week?"

She looked back down at her paperwork. "So you see my point."

Huyne was a little red in the face. I didn't figure on a guy who saw the kind of crime scenes he did being embarrassed at a little comment. But he was.

"Okay, don't help." He looked down. "And I'll do the same."

"Hold on. No need to be that way." I turned to look squarely at him. "You *could* look this up, this dancing business, so I've got to figure you're here for some bigger kind of something."

"I see. You're the perceptive type. Well, okay, Dane's already hired you to work on this, as I've been told. His lawyer's seen to it that I've got to work on it as well. Wouldn't it be better if we had a nice collaborative approach?"

I stared at him. "Dane and I have talked, but strictly speaking, he hasn't actually hired me yet. Still, collaboration is good. That's what you're offering?"

The single nod. "You tell me stuff; I tell you stuff."

I nodded slowly. "There would be the occasional confidentiality problem."

He sniffed. "Same here." He was looking at his glass, still turning it slowly. I poured him a little more.

I leaned forward with my elbows on the bar. "The tarantella is a dance that takes its name from Taranto, in the heel part of the Italian boot—or actually from a spider that is common to the area, the tarantula. At the time—post-Renaissance, I think—they thought the tarantula bite was poisonous and caused a disease called tarantism. The dance of the tarantella, get this, was actually supposed to be the *cure* for the disease. The music for the dance is in a compound double time—very fast, in other words—and the dance is very frenzied, and this somehow got the spider venom out. Also later, in the middle 1700s, there was a scientific treatise that very seriously put forth the the notion that all insects will dance rhythmically if you play them a tarantella."

He let out a breath and looked me in the eye. "How in the hell do you know all that?"

I glanced in Dally's direction. "Why won't anybody ever believe me when I say that I spend most of my time lying around doing nothing?" Back at Huyne.

"An idle mind is apparently, also an absorbent one. The tarantella? I read about it somewhere."

"Then what does the note mean to you"—he stared for another minute—"and your idle mind?"

I raised an eyebrow. "Well. Did you check the body for toxicological problems, for example?"

He shook his head. "Didn't seem like there was a need to since she died from being hanged."

"Maybe."

He leaned forward. "We'll check. Tarantula bite?"

"Naw. That's not really poisonous. Your black widow or your brown recluse can do some damage, but not the tarantula."

"Huh. So what's the pitch in the note then?"

I shrugged. "Maybe the murderer is an Arthur Murray instructor, or maybe they used some kind of poison to put Beth Dane out of commission before they actually hauled her up a lamppost. I mean, it's not something most people would do willingly, and the apron string was relatively tenuous."

Slow nodding. "I can see that. You'd have to knock out a person first. I can see that."

"Okay, your turn."

He put one elbow up on the bar and leaned his head in his hand. "My turn to what?"

"To tell me something. How's the Janey Finster case coming?"

"Fine. Solved. We arrested Mickey Nichols, as you know. We're pretty sure he did it." He squinted in my direction. "You knew Janey too, didn't you?"

"Yeah."

"Yeah." He deliberately looked away. "In fact there was talk that she was living with you when she got it."

"Unfounded. She just stayed with me when she needed to get away from it all."

"She got around."

I shook my head. "Not the way you mean. Foggy might have been pitching to her, and she might have been considering it, but ultimately she was always true to Mickey."

"In her fashion."

I nodded. "In her fashion."

"So why was she staying with you?"

I smiled. "I'm safe."

And God bless him, Huyne agreed. "I can see that. You could keep Mickey and Foggy away from her." Then he glanced at Dally. "And maybe you've got other things on your mind besides a skinny little kid on the outskirts of semiorganized crime."

"Lots of other things." I tilted my head. "So you're not investigating anything else about Janey then?"

He squinted. "No. Should we?"

"Just curious." I shook my head. "Like you said, I knew her." No point in telling him everything on our first date. Still, I couldn't resist messing with the situation a little. "It's just that Mick is more of a shoot-'em-up/blow-'em-down sort of a person, wouldn't you say? That's his rep, anyway. Don't figure on a guy like that smothering somebody. Janey was smothered, right?"

He gave a curt little jut of his chin. "She was found

smothered to death in her own bed with his prints all over her apartment."

"Smothered how?"

"With a pillow."

I slid off my barstool. "Doesn't sound like Mickey."

He seemed a little surprised at my abrupt movement and stood too. "Are we leaving?"

I rapped on the bar. "I'm seeing Ms. Oglethorpe home. I don't know what you're doing."

He took a long look at me, then let out a hefty breath. "Me? Well, I'm going back to the office." He started out the door. "I've suddenly got the idea I might open another damn case back up."

7

ARABESQUE

Taking Dally home always gave me the same feeling. Whether it was carrying her books for her in the sixth grade or driving her through the dark midtown streets, dog tired at four in the morning, I always felt complete.

I was driving. The moon was high. The world was quiet. Streetlights were on, house lights were off.

I turned down Penn. "I didn't tell you the oddest thing Mickey said."

She was slumped down beside me, eyes half open. "What was that?"

"He said he thought Beth was there at Foggy's New Year's Eve party with Joepye Adder."

She sat up a little. "What?"

"That's what he thought."

"Wow."

"Which, if it's true, makes two things I have to ask Joepye about."

She closed her eyes. "How do you know him anyway?"

I eased down to third, getting closer to her apartment. "You remember my pal Paul over at Tech? When Joepye was still teaching there, years ago, Paul introduced me. This was in the days before demon alcohol took ahold of Joe."

"They were friends?"

"Colleagues." I shook my head. "There's a diff in the world of academia."

"How?"

"Far as I can tell, colleagues lunch together, friends have dinner."

"I see."

I pulled up to the curb in front of the old house. I was just about to switch off the engine when I caught sight of a movement close to Dally's door. Somebody had ducked into the shadows on her porch.

I lowered my voice, kept the motor running. "You've got company."

She opened her eyes. "What?"

"Don't look now, but there's somebody hiding on your porch."

She couldn't resist sliding her eyes in the direction of her front door. "Wouldn't be the first time." Shook her head a little. "This neighborhood."

"You want to come back to my place?"

Eyes sliding back to me. "Have you vacuumed the sofa since Janey slept on it?"

"Oh." I looked back at the porch. "Look, could we deal with the intruder at your door before we get into your unwarranted jealousies?"

"I'm really tired. I'd like to sleep in my own bed. Just go kill that guy or shoo him away or something."

I opened the driver side door a little, took the rest of my keys from the one in the ignition so the car could stay running. "Look. Slide over here behind the wheel. If there's big trouble, just drive away."

"Yeah, like I'm about to drive away if you're in trouble."

"To go get help. You're the policeman's friend, remember?"

"Uh-huh."

I got out. She hesitated, but she knew I wouldn't move until she at least moved over behind the wheel. She did.

I buttoned my coat, pulled my hat down, and started for the porch. I waved at Dally bigger than I had to. "Thanks for the lift."

I turned to face the door and headed up the walk.

I could see the shadows shift. The figure was to my right, just beside the door. I fumbled loudly in my pocket for my keys, pulled them out, and bounded up the three steps to the porch.

Just as I hit the top step, I pulled the right half of my body back, cocked my right fist, and splayed two keys sticking out between my first two fingers. That way I could bust the nose and jab both eyes at the same time—if I had to.

The shadow moved back, and the voice made a little gasping noise.

I was practically on top of the guy before we got to a place where the streetlight spilled between the square columns and I could see the face.

I stopped and stood straight. "Damn it, Joepye."

"F-Flap?"

"Damn it. I could have put your eyes out."

He was breathing hard. "What the hell you come at me for?"

"How'd I know it was you?"

His voice was still a little high and strained. "Now who the hell else would be waiting for you at this time of night?"

"Waiting for me? This isn't my house."

"Don't I know, like, how you're a gentleman and all? And couldn't I figure you'd take Dally home most of the time, or something?"

I leaned in. "You've been drinking."

"Does the pope wear a funny hat?"

Dally couldn't sit still anymore, I guess. She started honking the horn and yelling, "Flap?"

"Shh." I stepped back over toward the car. "It's all right. It's Joepye."

She lowered her voice. "Speak of the devil."

I nodded.

She turned off the lights, then the engine.

I looked back at Joepye. "You were waiting for me? Here on Dally's porch?"

"That's right. I just got off working a little job sweeping up the post office back halls over there, and then I went and got me a little—"

"Joe"—you had to interrupt the guy—"why were you waiting for me?"

"I've got news."

"News?"

Dally was coming up the walk. "You two keep it down. People are trying to sleep all over the neighborhood."

I stared at Joepye. "What news, pal?"

"Found another dancer."

"What."

Dally was up the porch stairs, standing beside me, staring at the little guy in the dirty coat.

He smiled. "Hey, Dally."

"Hey, Joepye. Waiting to see me?"

"Naw. I was waiting for Flap. I got news."

I squinted at him. I was afraid I knew what he was going to say. "What do you mean, another dancer?"

He shifted his weight and tried to focus on us. "Why do you think I'm up drunk this late? There's another girl, Flap. Hanging from a light over there, just around the corner."

8

THE TANGO

When you know you're walking to a place where there's a dead girl swinging from a lamppost, the whole world takes on a certain angularity—like a Fritz Lang movie. I'm saying the old familiar neighborhood was something out of a black-and-white silent movie about the horror of the human condition.

Despite the suspicions, the questions I had for my companion, we didn't talk. The whole scene demanded silence.

We rounded Penn, right on Tenth, and even from a couple blocks away, I could see her silhouette. As we got closer, the harsh downlight made it impossible to tell what her face looked like. I was glad of that.

We got within a few feet and stopped.

I stared up. "Well, you were right. There's absolutely a dead girl hanging there."

He nodded. "Note on her too. Just like the last one."

I squinted. "Yup."

He looked at me. "You think you'll get this one down or let her come down on her own, like the last one?"

I shook my head. "All I'm doing is standing here until the police come."

He cocked his head. "You think the police know about this?"

I looked down the empty streets. "They do now. Dally called them."

"What? When?"

"Just now. When we left."

"How you know that?"

"I asked her to, but I think she would have done it anyway. We're getting to know the detective who's handling the other one, the other case like this."

"That Huymish guy?"

"Burnish Huyne."

"That's a name."

I smiled. "Look who's talking."

He didn't smile back. "What in this world you want with the police? You're the one who gets all the spooky messages just by staring at nothing. You're the one who can figure it out. The police, all they want is to close the case so they can go home. They don't care a thing about it. They just want to run you in for doing nothing."

I shook my head. "I know your association with the police hasn't been the finest—"

His voice rose a little. "They just want to run you in for nothing!"

I looked up at the girl again. "You ever had any trouble with the cops while you were still at Tech?"

"At Tech?"

"When you were teaching at Tech?"

He looked at me like he was looking through a window shade. "I don't remember that. That wasn't me. I wasn't there."

"Okay."

When you drink a lot for a long, long time, you can seem like you're fairly sober, sound like it too, but when it comes to facing anything like the truth about who you are and what you are, it all gets fuzzy and the center will not hold. Mr. Adder had largely been in charge of a set of glorified shop courses in another life. He'd understood the basic patterns of electricity. It seemed to me, there in the light of the lamp, in the shadow of its strange fruit, that somehow odd patterns of electricity had become a way of life for him.

He was beginning to rant. "I mean it. Why'd you call the cops? Damn it, Flap! I just wanted to show this to you. Now I got to leave."

My voice was even. "Why do you have to leave?"

He turned a chilly eye my way. "I need another run-in with the police?"

"Why did you come get me?"

"What? Why'd I come get you? So you could . . ." But he momentarily lost track of what he was saying.

I locked eyes with him. "So I could what?"

He squeezed his eyes shut and concentrated. "So *you* could get the next note off the body and find out more what happened to Mr. Dane's little niece—no cops." He opened his eyes. They were softer than they had been. "Beth. She's a sweet kid. Real smart."

"Was, Joe."

He squeezed his eyes shut again, trying to get it all straight. "Yeah." Big exhale. "Was."

I could see the car coming. I tapped his elbow. "Cops. You care to split?"

He looked. "Naw, damn. They seen me now. Damn it, Flap. Why'd you call?"

The searchlight hit us. The voice was iron. "Please place your hands in plain sight where we can see them."

We did. I held mine out, like welcoming an old friend. Joepye held his up, like he was standing at gunpoint.

The voice from the car was no less hard. "Tucker?"

I managed a smile. "That's me."

"Detective Huyne is on the way."

The searchlight stayed on us, but the two cops got out of the car. The one who came from the passenger side nodded at my sidekick.

"Joepye."

Joe didn't look the guy in the eye. "So?"

"You found this one?"

He looked at me. "Flap found her. I just happened to see her here as I was, you know, what you call passing by on my way home."

The other officer snarled a little laugh. "And just where would that be at this point? Home?"

I let my hands fall slowly to my side. "Joe here is like the lilies of the field."

The first officer shook his head. "Isn't joepye a weed?"

Joe was very affable under the circumstances. He smiled at the officer. "It's got a pretty flower, though."

I added my two cents. "It's a staple in some wildflower gardens."

The other officer patted himself obscenely. "Staple this."

Joe and I both knew better than to respond.

I stared up at the girl. "There's something really . . . the apron string/noose thing is really something."

Joepye nodded. "They say it's Freudian."

"Who says that?"

He inclined his head. "I heard some cop say it."

I looked over at the officers. "Is that right? You guys read a lot of Freud, do you?"

Joepye looked down. "Maybe it was Mr. Dane who said it."

I nodded. "More likely." I stared again. "But that's not it—not entirely. It's like there's something familiar about it."

Joepye lowered his voice. "Familiar?"

"Like a dream image, or a . . . something."

His voice was even more hushed. "You do your thing already?"

"My thing? No. This is something else."

The passenger side officer interrupted. "Would it be all right with you two if you'd just shut up until Detective Huyne got here?"

It wasn't really a question.

We stood in silence under the silver water of light the moon had ladled out over everything. Pale faces just outside the pool of artificial luminescence. No one wanted to stand directly under the body.

I don't think it was more than five minutes before Huyne showed up.

He'd come from the opposite direction, so he parked his station wagon facing the other car, headlight to headlight.

He hauled himself out of his ride. "Mr. Tucker."

"Detective Huyne."

Huyne blinked at Joepye. "Mr. Adder."

"Hey."

"You're actually the one who spotted the body first?"

He looked down. "I don't know."

"You went to get Tucker."

"I did. I wasn't sure what I saw." He finally looked up at Huyne and grinned. "I might have been drinking just a little."

Huyne smiled back, but it wasn't a friendly smile at all. "So you went to Tucker to see if he could tell you what this was?"

Joepye nodded slowly. "I think that was it."

Huyne looked up at the body. "What else could this have been besides a body, Joepye?"

Joepye didn't look. "Sometimes the kids'll tie some shoes together and sling them over street wires or lampposts."

"Shoes?"

"Or it could have been a squirrel's nest. They get real big."

"On a lamppost?"

Joepye was getting agitated again. "How'd I know it was a lamppost? Didn't I just say I was drinking. Hell, it could have been a dogwood or a phone pole or a basketball hoop." He cocked his head defiantly. "I need glasses too, you know. I'm drunk and I need glasses. So."

The detective took a long look and then shrugged in my direction. "Mr. Tucker? Does that look like a dead body to you?"

I nodded. "Does to me."

He looked at the other two cops. "We have a confirmation. Would you two mind getting the ladder out of my wagon?"

The two uniforms fetched an extension ladder.

Huyne directed. "All I want to do is take a look at the note. I'd like to try to leave everything like it is, but if I could just see what the note on this one says—"

I piped up. "You noticed that."

He nodded. "Yeah. I figured we could get started right away thinking about the information on the note. Thinking's not going to disturb the crime scene. Would that be all right with you?"

I nodded right back. "I was a little curious about that myself."

One held the ladder while the other clambered up it.

The man at the top of the ladder stared at the note for a minute and then called down. "It just says, 'Number Two: The Tango.' Can I come down?"

Huyne looked up at him. "Yeah. Come on down."

He did. It was Huyne's turn to stare at me. "So?"

I was looking up at the body. "I was just thinking how nice and organized it is when a serial killer actually numbers the victims."

Huyne nodded. "Numbers and titles."

"Right."

"So what does it mean?"

I looked at him. "Just like that? Right away I'm supposed to know what it means?"

He squinted. "What do you know about the tango?"

"It was born in Argentina—in brothels. It was basically copulation set to music. Or foreplay anyway. Very popular in America in the twenties. Had a post–World War Two nostalgic resurgence. And then it finally got what it deserved from Bertolucci."

"The filmmaker?"

"*Last Tango in Paris*. If you've ever seen it, you can't think of the dance without also thinking of odd uses for butter."

He had no idea. "I see. So what does all this mean?"

"That the murderer is from Argentina, born in the

twenties, fought in World War Two, and hates Marlon Brando."

He was willing to play. "Or loves Maria Schneider. Wasn't that the actress's name?" So maybe he did have an idea.

I nodded.

He shrugged. "You can shut up now, but give it some thought, okay?"

I looked at him sideways. "Why are you being so . . ."

"Cooperative? Helpful with your . . . investigation? Even nice?" He took a step closer to me and lowered his voice. "Well, I'm not doing it entirely for you, see? Ms. Oglethorpe is something of a favorite around our station house, as you may already have discovered."

The way he said Dally's name—even her last name—told me more about him than the note told me about the stiff.

"I see." I nodded. "Well, I'll tell her you said hey. I can go?"

Big nod from him. "Please."

I almost took a step. "Joepye can go?"

He stared at the little guy for a minute. "I don't think so. He found the body—again. I need to talk to him awhile."

"As a matter of fact"—I didn't move—"I'd like to talk with him too, now that you mention it."

He shook his head. "Not tonight, Flap. Go on, now." He flipped his hand away.

Can't say I liked being shooed like a dog.

Still, I started the walk back to Dally's place, where my car was parked.

Lot himself was wiser, but I followed the example of Lot's wife. I turned around to take one last look at the poor kid hanging from the lamppost. Good thing I did. I suddenly remembered where I knew that image from, long before all this mess started.

9

LOBSTER WALK

"Who is it?" She was trying to make her voice sound as tough and irritated as possible.

I was in no mood. "Who else would be knocking on your door at this time of night?"

The door swung open. She was already in the black kimono she usually wore for a bathrobe. She was smiling, but it was one you might file under the "wan" category. "I just didn't want it to be Joepye again, sneaking up on my porch."

"Oh, he'll be out of your hair for a while. He's being entertained by the police."

She closed the door behind me. "I see. I take it the police didn't find you as entertaining as he is."

"Right. So guess why am I here."

"Long night, and you need a little mint tea?" She

waved the mug in her hand. "I'm just getting some for myself."

I nodded. "Peppermint tea. Very calming."

We shuffled into the kitchen. She pulled down another mug. "So why *are* you here?"

"Gérard de Nerval."

"What?" The kettle started whistling. She look it off the heat and poured into both mugs.

"French literary figure. Nerval lived in Paris in the early 1800s, but he was the Salvador Dali of his day. He had all these surreal absinthe hallucinations, and he wrote about them. I think the book's called *Le Chimera* or *Les Chimères* or something. Very strange guy. He used to walk a lobster on a leash down the Champs-Élysées."

"No kidding." She handed me the tea and sat at her kitchen table. Her kitchen was more spacious than mine and filled with plants, mostly fresh herbs growing in clay pots. She didn't do much cooking, but when she did, you could alert the media, and five stars wouldn't be enough to put beside the menu. Five *shooting* stars, maybe.

"Gérard de Nerval," I said again.

"Sounds familiar. I guess you've mentioned him before." She closed her eyes for a second. "Anyway, you bring him up because this is a strange, surreal night, what with the scary visitor on my porch and the dead body hanging in the park. I assume there actually was one."

"Assume away. But that's not why I bring him up.

It's more specific than that. He was, as you might imagine, a very troubled soul—"

"Wait." She raised her eyebrows. "He's the one that wrote the translation of *Faust* that Berlioz used for his opera."

See why I love her? I had to smile. "Correct. You should be on *Jeopardy*."

"Okay, now I know the guy you mean. Just took me a minute."

"Yeah." I sat at the table with her. "But do you want me to tell you the story or not?"

"Story?"

"Of why I bring him up in the first place—on a night like this."

"Oh." She nodded. "Yes, I guess I do want that. The story."

I set down my mug a little noisily. "How do you suppose good old Gérard de Nerval died?"

"Tell me."

"Suicide."

She cocked her head. "Yes?"

"He hanged himself from a lamppost"—I leaned forward—"using his mother's apron—by the neck from a lamppost with an apron string. That's how he died."

"Oh, yeah, you *have* told me this before." She stared silently.

I blinked. "Didn't you hear what I said?"

"I did hear what you said." She took another sip. "Now listen to what I have to say. The person that's doing this—this hanging these kids like this—is possessed of some pretty eclectic esoterica: a knowledge of the tarantella and some French nutcase, not to mention an ability to whisk somebody up a lamppost and not have anybody see him. I mean, that's quite a populated neighborhood where he's strung these two girls up. Lots of people could see, even this time of night."

I yawned. "I know." That's all I could manage.

She smiled back. "Okay, that proves my point. What we both really need is *sleep*."

I nodded. "I'd say you're right. But you're also right about the murderer: He's got odd knowledge, he's nuts, and he doesn't care."

She took the cups and put them in the sink. She had her back to me. "Flap?"

"Um-hm?"

"You wouldn't want to grab your shut-eye on my sofa here tonight, would you?"

I looked at the top of her kitchen table. Didn't know where else to look. "Don't see why not. It's closer than my apartment, isn't it?"

She nodded, still not turning to face me. "By a couple of steps, yeah, probably is."

My voice was soft. "Still a little shaken by strange men lurking on your porch?"

"A little." She turned her profile. "I like to know the men lurking on my porch."

I nodded. "Right. Okay. I'll stay."

She started out of the room. "You know where everything is. I'll make a nice egg white omelet in the morning."

I got up. "I hope you've got espresso beans."

She didn't move. "I do."

I stood beside her in the doorframe. Her face was very close to mine. "You do?"

She turned, but her eyes were down. "You know, that wasn't much of a story . . . about Nerval."

I brushed a strand of her hair back behind her ear. "Well, maybe *story* wasn't the right word."

"So I guess this is good night."

I dropped my hand to my side. Her arm was touching mine. "I guess. Although I could stand right here just like this for another hour and a half or so."

She finally looked up. "Flap . . ."

But I wouldn't let her finish the thought. "See, if my name were almost anything else, it wouldn't have ruined the effect of a perfectly good romantic mood like this. But it's a challenge to maintain the romance when you've got to softly whisper a moniker like mine."

"Okay." She smiled, looked away, and moved out of the doorframe. "See you in the morning."

She knew I was nodding, even though she wasn't looking back.

10

SHOW DOG STATUS

Much as I wanted to sleep in the next morning, that's how much the person pounding on the door wanted me to get up. Pounding. Like with the back part of the fist, not a little knuckle rap.

So despite my ire, I put on a happy face, flung myself unsteadily up, straightened my clothes as much as possible, and went to the door.

Huyne seemed surprised to see me. "Jesus. Tucker."

I nodded. "Detective."

"Well"—he stared—"looks like you slept in your clothes."

I tried not to yawn. "I did."

"Here?"

"Uh-huh." I don't know why I didn't just say I'd slept on the sofa.

He looked past me into the place. "Ms. Oglethorpe here?"

"She's still asleep. She works nights. What time is it anyway?"

He glanced at his watch. "About ten."

I still didn't invite him in, which he clearly wanted me to do, what with the anxious body language and the peering over my shoulder into the darkened room. "Seems a little early for you too, considering how late you were out last night."

He got my eye. "A little. But I've got this work to do, see."

"And you need to see Ms. Oglethorpe."

"I do."

"Do you mind my asking what for?"

"I don't mind your asking as long as you don't mind my not telling you."

I smiled. "So I guess we're even." I stood aside, finally. "Like to come in?"

He made a little snorting noise, like a riled animal. Then he brushed past me into the living room.

I watched him invade. "I thought we were supposed to be friends, at least in this particular endeavor."

He looked back at me over his shoulder. "Well, I was kind of operating along those lines myself. Then I start thinking."

"That's a mistake."

"Yeah. Still, here's what I'm thinking: You and that

little ratweed Joepye are the first ones there both times we find dead girls hanging in the park. And then you seem to know the answers to all my questions. So I get to thinking, *What is it that looks like a mutt, smells like a mutt, but acts like a show dog?*"

I cocked my head. "I just woke up. I'm not in the mood for riddles."

He squinted back at me, hard. "Then I'll tell you the answer. The answer is: It's a mutt that wants you to think it's something else."

I shifted my weight. "Now, last night you shooed me away from what they call the crime scene like a stray, and this morning you come lumbering into somebody else's house and impugn my show dog status." I took a step in his direction. "I sense a change in our relationship. I think I'm entitled to know why this has happened. I thought we had such a nice date at Easy last night."

He took a little step my way. "I'll tell you what happened." He held up his hand and counted off the troubles on his fingers. "One, I find out you had a conversation with Mick Nichols in my very own establishment, and this man is not only no good but also a murderer; I still think that no matter what other confusing information you send my way. And then, two, I find out that he gets you to help him prove he didn't kill a girl that I'm pretty sure he did. Okay? Then, three, I find you are a font of information about unusual old dances, and you don't look much like a dancer to me. But the kicker is four: Joepye Adder tells me that he thinks *you're* the one who's killing these girls."

"Comedy's supposed to come in threes, pal. And what you're telling, whether you realize it or not, is a joke."

Not that Huyne would believe it, but that Joepye would say it—that was the surprise. Joe must have been put under some severe stress.

He leaned toward me. "Yeah?"

"Well . . . you don't even remotely agree with him about that last wild allegation, do you?"

He stared at me a second longer, then let go. "No. I don't. But I've got to ask myself why he said it."

I rubbed my eyes. "Could it be, Detective Huyne, that your police techniques might have led the poor guy to say things he thought you were wanting to hear?"

He made that sound again. "That little sucker is tougher than you think."

I shook my head. "I know he's tough. I also know he's easily confused. Did you ask him how many of the girls he'd killed himself?"

He looked at the floor. "Yeah, well, he did admit that he'd killed them both."

"Ask him where Hoffa is, by any chance?"

That got him. He finally cracked open a tiny smile. "I'm sure he'd tell me."

I finally moved into the living room. "So why the hard sell?"

He looked out the window. "Would you believe me if I said it was my job?"

"No." I watched him move slowly around the room. "There's more to it than that."

He turned to look at me. "Okay, here's the deal." Deep breath. "I was surprised to see you here, and it irritated me, and I came on a little harsh because that was my first reaction. I'm not proud of it. It just happened."

"You're an emotional boy."

He sniffed. "Not usually." He looked around the room. "I thought you two were just friends."

"There's nothing *just* about our thing." I held a steady look. "It's more in the *what-the-hell-is-this* category."

"I see." He looked away.

"Well, you probably really don't see."

His voice was small. "Yeah. Maybe I don't."

He actually jumped when he heard Dally's voice coming from the stairs.

"What's all this noise? Where's my beauty sleep?"

I looked up. She was dressed, which said to me that she'd heard most of the conversation and had decided to get made up for her guest. What · *that* meant, I had no idea.

He was the first to answer. "Ms. Oglethorpe."

She came down the stairs and into the room. "Hey, boys. Coffee?"

I smiled. "You all can have that weak American brown water—"

She wouldn't let me finish. "I know what you want."

She made it sound more suggestive than she needed to. Once again I was at a loss as to what that meant.

We followed her to the kitchen. She went about making two separate versions of the coffee beverage and assumed the hostess role with the kind of ease that made her the perfect bar owner.

"Detective Huyne? You think Flap killed those little girls?"

He tapped on the top of the table with this fingers. I interpreted it as a nervous habit. "The point is, I have to explore every alleyway, see?"

She started the little espresso machine. "Well, that one's a dead end, don't you think?"

He lifted his eyes to me. "Tucker here was just saying I think too much."

She nodded. "That's his party line."

I was still trying to figure why he'd shifted in his attitude toward me in under twenty-four hours. Usually takes me a good week to offend people like him.

It seemed to me that Dally had sensed it as well and had determined to talk to the guy so that I could observe. Or maybe I was reading something into that. I was left wondering what had happened to my good old intuition. Seemed out of whack, or maybe it was just that I hadn't had my morning pot of espresso.

Dally pointed, and we all sat at the kitchen table. "So what is the actual purpose of this visit, then, do you think?"

He breathed out. "I partly wanted to see if you were all right. Joepye said he scared you last night."

She kept a steady eye on him. "It wasn't that bad."

He couldn't keep up his stare and looked over in the direction of the noise from the espresso machine. "It wasn't just that." He started to talk, then stopped, then looked at me. "The kid we found last night? The stiff? The victim?"

I nodded, staring pretty hard at him myself. "I remember."

He nodded a little. "Well . . ." he looked back at Dally ". . . she was your neighbor. She lived upstairs in the other half of this house."

11

STRANGE FRUIT

There were only three apartments in the old house. We knew who he was talking about.

Dally took it hard. "Minnie?"

Minnie Moran was just a kid, in school studying to be an artist. She was somebody you'd notice on the street—a blond knockout who was always singing old jazz tunes, smiling at strangers, addicted to espresso and good cheer.

I stifled my impulse to take Dally's hand in front of Huyne and looked at him instead. "You're certain about this?"

He nodded my way. "And then what with Joepye creeping around and you being here—to the untrained observer, this could all look very suspicious."

I sat back. "But you see through all that."

"I do, but you don't understand the pressure I can get from my captain. Not to mention that this mess is starting to attract the media. I mean, national media. It's a hell of a story, I guess."

Dally still hadn't gotten past the shock of the news. "Minnie was just in this kitchen yesterday. I lent her twenty bucks to buy charcoal for her second life class over at the college."

I tried to smile at Huyne. "Don't you think it would be best if somebody—some squad car—could hang around this general area for a while, kind of keep an eye on things. I don't much care for the coincidence . . ."

But I didn't have to finish. Huyne knew exactly what coincidence I was talking about, and just exactly what to do. "Already have a twenty-four watch."

I nodded. "Whole neighborhood."

"Right."

I looked at Dally. "Okay, let me slam down a little of that espresso and be off. I have errands."

She knew what I meant. "Okay." She got up, still not herself. "Thanks for staying last night, by the way. That sofa's not the most comfortable."

And yet again, was she saying that to apologize to me for the condition of the couch or to assure Huyne that I had rested my bones downstairs? I took in a slow, deep breath, thinking how I needed my psyche adjusted, and me without the number of a good psychic chiropractor.

She'd filled a demitasse, nearly to the rim after dumping in two good lumps of brown sugar. I took the cup from her hand. She looked me in the eye. And there it was: the look I'd been hoping for. It was the look that said, "I know what you've got to do and where you're going now, and I'll keep this rube occupied while you do it." Good. Made the espresso go down a lot smoother.

So I drained the cup, set it down delicately, and stood. "Okay, I'm off."

Huyne was a little skeptical of my sudden departure. "Where're you off to all of a sudden?"

I smiled at him. "You don't seem to understand what a busy, busy man I am. I currently have two clients, and I have not done one whit of work on their behalf. I must away."

He gave me the steel stare, but he let it go. "Nothing out of town, I hope."

I straightened my tie. "Subtle." I turned to Dally. "Don't bother seeing me to the door."

She widened her eyes for a split second, and I skimmed the floor of the kitchen in two steps.

The sun was dodging behind some hefty dark clouds. I knew that I ought to dash homeward for an umbrella and a shave—not to mention a change and a shower—but I was suddenly feeling urgent about my work. Gets like that sometimes; you can't be bothered with hygiene when the wheels of the world are turning.

As I got in the car, I glanced up at the window that looked out from Minnie's living room. I hadn't been up there since a party the previous summer, but I remembered the swell self-portrait on the wall and the tasty spinach and water chestnut dip. Minnie had been a senior at the Atlanta College of Art, a photographer. Her big show, which Dally and I had seen just the past Christmas, had been a series of staged images from songs by Billie Holiday—very clever. Each photo had a small CD player in front of it, softly playing the song that the image had come from. The speakers had been remarkably directional, so you could hear the song only when you were standing right in front of the picture it pertained to, which had made it all seem very intimate.

The series had included one of the few songs Billie had written herself, "Strange Fruit," about lynchings. A classic. The image for that song in Minnie's show had been a picture of the artist herself, dressed like Christ, hanging by the neck from a blooming dogwood tree.

12

RAT HEAVEN

Less than ten minutes later I was pounding on Dane's front door. He came, finally, dressed in a serious burgundy house coat, like the kind you might see older gentlemen in Victorian England wear around the parlor.

He seemed surprised to see me. "Mr. Tucker?"

I brushed past him and walked into his foyer. "Your niece is now officially part of a trend."

"What?" He closed the door.

"We found another body last night. Same deal."

"Same deal?" His head was cocked at what looked to be a painful angle.

I chose my words. "Joepye Adder and I found another girl, about the same age as your niece, hanging from another lamppost in the park just a few hours ago, and she was hanging by an apron string—again."

His face was white. "How can this be true?"

"We know who the girl was too. Not a prostitute. An art student. She lived upstairs from Ms. Oglethorpe."

"She lived . . ." But he couldn't seem to finish the sentence.

So I did it for him. "Upstairs from Ms. Oglethorpe. I'm not going to waste your time telling you how increasingly personal that makes this mess. But make your retainer check out to Flap Tucker in the amount of twenty-five hundred bucks."

He looked toward the kitchen. "I think I need more coffee."

I nodded. "I could do with a glass of water."

We made it to the kitchen.

Before he was even in his seat, I pressed on. "I'd like to get into your niece's apartment or room or whatever. I think now would be a good time for me to admit I'm actually working on this situation with you and get to the discovery of what they sometimes call clues in the genre."

"What are you talking about?" He stared.

"I want to get into your niece's place. Do you have the address? Do you have a key? Could you come along with me, as nearest of kin, and go through her stuff?" I blinked. "These, I believe, are my questions at the moment."

"I know the address." He took a sip of his coffee. "Or I have the address. I don't have a key. But I'd be happy to go with you." He sipped again. "Or at least I'd be willing to go." He set the cup down. "You want to go now."

I nodded. "I want to go yesterday."

"I'll be a moment. I have to get out of the computer, and I need to put on some clothes."

Without another word, he was gone up the stairs.

I took my time, looked about the place. It was what they like to call well appointed. I couldn't be certain because it was up high on the wall, but I thought the Picasso might have been a signed original instead of a print.

When he came back downstairs, Dane had on an obviously expensive sweater, dress slacks, and some painful-looking loafers.

He handed me a check. "Shall we?"

I nodded and pocketed the retainer.

The drive to Hepzibah's place didn't take long. She lived on a dead-end street off Eleventh. The sign was missing, so I had no idea what we might call the street where she lived. I only knew that it was so much less fashionable than Dane's address that it might as well have been in another city.

Barely out of the car, Dane pointed up to a window. "That's her place, up there. Everything in the building is locked up tightly." He shot me a look. "But I assume a man of your occupation has a way with locked doors."

As if in answer to his comment, I produced a barely visible hex wrench, fiddled with the front door for exactly three seconds, and opened the door for him.

He smiled and went in first.

Up the stairs, the kid's door still had a plastic Christmas wreath on it and yellow police tape across the frame. As it turned out, that door was trickier. The doorknob turned easily enough, but the door was clearly locked somehow from the inside.

I turned to Dane. "Would anybody else be here, do you know?"

"I wouldn't know. I don't think she had a roommate."

I shrugged and tapped the door with a fair amount of authority. No answer.

"Another way in?" I asked.

"I don't think so, but then, once again . . ."

"Wait here then, would you?" I pushed past him in the narrow corridor.

Outside I shoved through some fairly difficult ivy and a rat's heaven of garbage to the back of the house. There was an old-fashioned trellis, just like they have in the movies, covered with kudzu.

I took only a second to consider the little spot, but it occurred to me that it had likely been a pretty nice old house in its day—probably the twenties—and that trellis might once have held roses or even bougainvillaea that someone had cared about. But by the end of the twentieth century it was just another midtown litter-strewn hooker barn. I wondered if the ghosts of the people whose garden it had been were ever abroad of a midnight hour, visiting the old neighborhood, staring, like me, up at the kudzu.

The moment passed, and I vaulted up the trellis, just close enough to the back window of the kid's apartment to make it tantalizing. I made quite a racket getting up. If there had been anybody home in the building, he would doubtless have heard me, but nobody appeared, so I assumed the whole place was vacant.

The window was locked, but that was no challenge; you just slide a sturdy piece of thin metal between the upper and lower parts and turn the crank. Easy to unlock—and lock—from the outside, if you think of it. Only took a little effort because the frame was warped. I got the window open and flung myself in.

The apartment was dark. The room into which I had fallen was the bathroom. I added to the general noise I had already made by tumbling over everything on the toilet back and the sink. It was the smallest bathroom I'd ever been in, and black as a dungeon.

"Hello?" Thought I ought to check again. "It's the Fuller Brush Man." Like anybody her age would even know what that was.

I peered through the bathroom door. It opened into her bedroom. The bed was a mess, and the room was a little stuffy, but nothing was really amiss. I took a few steps into the room, cast my eye about. Only one thing on the wall caught my eye: a framed photograph. I was about to look closer, because I had the feeling I'd seen it before, when someone cleared his throat.

It was Dane shuffling around, so I gathered that the hallway was right outside the next room, which, as it turned out, was the only other room in the apartment.

The shades were up in there, so I could see better. There was a television on top of another television, a kitchen alcove with a poster for *The Wizard of Oz* up over the stove, a wooden table with three legs and a mannequin's arm for the fourth. On the table were the barely recognizable remains of a breakfast someone had fixed maybe a month before, and plenty of roaches still taking advantage of their good fortune. They were crawling all over some charcoal sketches of nudes that were lying on the table to get to the cereal.

In fact the roaches barely took any notice of me at all. No scurrying away because some giant human had come crashing into the room. These were roaches with confidence of ownership. Just ignore the big man. He's only a visitor.

I made it to the front door and saw immediately the access problem: It was padlocked from the inside.

"Dane?"

"You're inside."

"Right. Hang on a second." I slipped another little metal gizmo into the padlock, fiddled a little, and the thing gave up.

I opened the door. "Won't you come in?"

He didn't smile. He just stepped past the police

tape and gave a glancing examination of the whole place. Then he made his pronouncement.

"God in heaven."

I shrugged. "I've seen worse. Lots worse."

"I suppose. But did your favorite niece live there?"

Not having a niece of any sort, except unless you count Dally's little niece up in Black Pine Mountain, Georgia, or a couple of hayseed namesakes of ours down Tifton way, I kept my mouth shut.

"What am I here for, again?" He sounded irritated.

"To see what you can see." I looked around. "Like, for instance . . ." I paused just long enough for a kind of dramatic effect I suddenly wanted to have on the guy. "I didn't notice, as I passed through the bedroom, the Raggedy Ann doll you mentioned the other day." I watched his face for signs of anything strange. "Wouldn't she have it sitting on her bed? Isn't that the way kids do?"

"Well," he began, his voice betraying nothing, "I'd like to think she loved it as much as that, but it is possible, of course, that it didn't mean as much to her as I thought it did."

"Let's look anyway."

He nodded. We went into the bedroom, flipped on the light, and gave it a good once-over. Depressing primarily in its minimalism, the room gave up no clues about anything—except that life can be fairly tough on some kids when it wants to be. No mystery there.

And no doll.

I turned to him. "No doll at all."

He didn't look at me. I pressed. "Would she have hocked it, do you think?"

He raised his head a little. "What pawnshop would offer her any money for a flimsy old rag doll?"

"Don't reckon they'd know its value?"

He shook his head. "Not likely, would you say? Sotheby's maybe, but not a pawnbroker."

"I think you're right." I smiled at him, then let the full import of my suspicions flood my tone of voice. "I just wanted to know what *you* thought."

"What I thought?" He finally looked me in the eye. Then, as if he'd heard me on a three-second delay: "Oh."

"Oh"—I looked at him sideways—"what?"

"Oh, this: You had it in your mind that I might have come over here before now and looked for the doll or even gotten the doll—something of that sort."

"Not exactly." I kept my gaze evenly locked with his. "I just thought it was a little, how shall we say, *obvious* that you mentioned the doll the other day at Mary Mac's. It seemed to be—I don't know—pointed or leading or . . . something."

"I don't know what you mean."

"I mean that when someone hires me or wants to hire me to find something, they hardly ever go right to the specifics. They start with the big picture, and the details are things I have to pry out, like gold from the mountainside. You gave me a little chunk of gold without my even having to ask. I was worried about it because it was too easy. I was also a little worried about your whimsical 'I want to know *why*' speech."

His voice was calm. "Why were you worried about that?"

"Because it sounded too much like something *I* might say."

"I see." He sat down on his niece's bed, his voice changed completely. "Well, you'll have to make up your mind. Either you're disturbed by my being too specific, or you're worried by my being too academic. You can't have your Kate and Edith too."

I stared for a second. "Well, you certainly are one strange old bird, wouldn't you say?"

"I am."

"Okay, since it's all out in the open, what's the deal with the doll?"

"Absolutely nothing—if it were here."

"Now you're just being obtuse. Or is that isosceles?"

"Do you know," he said, "why I'm the best bass player in the region?"

"Practice?"

"Everyone practices. I prepare. I order scores months before a concert, study them, find inconsistencies in the notation, ask questions about the composer. What time of day was he born? What were his eating habits? Same for the conductor, any new guest conductor—what are his quirks? I anticipate them."

"So"—I thought I knew where he was going— "you mean you were trying to anticipate something about your niece's . . . situation. Something about the doll. But what would it mean if the doll weren't here?"

"It's *not* here."

"Thanks for reminding us of the obvious. Question stands: So what?"

"It's the only thing she owned of any value whatsoever," he told me impatiently. "Naturally it's a pivotal issue, a motive. One of her slummy friends saw it and killed her for it."

Rich people. They think everything pivots on dough. So naturally Dane would think the scratch was the issue. I felt I ought, strictly as a public service, to set him straight.

"Let me just count the ways you're wrong. First, despite your worldview, a thing like this is never about money; second, money—while being in fact the root of all evil—is not at the root of all things, and by the way, didn't we just decide that most people wouldn't recognize the value of the thing anyway? And three, murder and suicide are both generally emotional issues. Passion, not cash. You have taken yourself on something of a wild-goose chase. You have caught yourself something of a red herring."

"Are you finished?"

"Let's see . . . geese, fish—care to hear something in a 'blind alley' phrase?"

"What clues did *you* come here looking for then?"

"That's just the thing," I explained, looking around the room again. "I try never to come into a situation like this one with any preconceptions at all. I try to let the clues find me, rather than the other way around."

"How often does that work?" His voice was dripping, but I couldn't decide if disdain was the predominant chord, or only irony.

So I stared him in the eye again. "Every time."

He didn't blink. "Still, the doll's not here. Is it." Not a question.

13

ZEN PUNCH LINE #13

"So the doll wasn't there? So what?"

Dally was still pacing. She'd been doing it since I'd returned from Beth's apartment.

"That's not the point, pal. The point is, the place was all locked up from the inside. Something Dane didn't even comment on."

"Oh." She stopped. "Right. But was it because he was so focused on the money thing or because he already knew it would be locked from the inside?"

"Exactly." I nodded. "I don't trust him for half a measure."

"I was wondering when we'd get around to the musical metaphors."

"Oh." I leaned forward, "You're going to fault me for a little in-keeping-with-the-situation phrase?"

"So why'd you leave the kid's place so quickly?"

I sat back into the sofa. Dally's sofa is alive. You lean back, it embraces you, and you feel comforted. I sighed.

"Well"—my eyes half closed—"just as we were going to give the outer room a good going-over, we heard people rousing themselves downstairs. Apparently they'd been there all the time, although it was hard for me to believe that my racket hadn't piqued their interest before."

"I guess when your upstairs neighbor is a streetwalker, you get used to a little ambient chaos." She disappeared into the kitchen.

"I guess. So Dane beat it out the front door, I clicked the padlock, shimmied down the trellis in the back, and we were gone before the guys downstairs had a chance to heat up their first shots of the day."

"Junkies?"

"What crackhead's going to sleep through all that noise? I'm telling you I could have waked the dead, maybe did. Only junkies can sleep like that."

"Okay, so what was the point of going over there, again?"

I closed my eyes completely. "(A) To fit Dane into the picture, (B) to check for clues like a real detective, (C) to get the lay of the land."

Her head poked out of the kitchen. "Explain C."

"Is this neighborhood the center point, or is it the park?"

"What do you mean?"

"My fear"—I opened my eyes—"was that Beth's

place was somehow close by here and that the person who's hoisting up these women to give them dancing lessons is just grabbing anybody in your neighborhood."

"Oh." Merest of pauses. "And?"

"And Beth's place is like another part of town. Close to here geographically, yeah, but it's another world, economically or . . . socially. I mean, junkies and hookers and bikers and rats. Not someplace you'd just casually wander to from here. You know how Midtown is."

"Which makes the park"—she went back into the kitchen—"the actual territory de crime."

"Check." I slouched. "But there's more."

"Such as," she called, invisibly.

"Such as a photo on her bedroom wall that looked, I think, like the work of your recently deceased upstairs neighbor."

Silence.

"Dally?"

She reappeared. "One of Minnie's photographs was up in Dane's niece's apartment?"

"That's what it looked like to me, at first glance. Also there were charcoal sketches—like an art student might draw."

She just stood there.

I watched her for a moment, then spoke right up again. "As long as you're doing your impersonation of the baffled club owner, tell me what's wrong with what I've said about the kid's apartment so far."

"What are you asking me?"

"The place was locked from the inside—door and window."

"Like you said."

"And there was police tape across the front . . ." I waited.

Her eyes grew wide. "Are you saying that the police haven't been inside her apartment yet?"

"It's not likely they got in and out the same way I did."

"Wouldn't they have just busted in?"

I shrugged. "Maybe. Or maybe they didn't want to disturb the scene, as they say. Huyne seems like a stickler to me. I guess it could be that the boys in blue found the place, couldn't get in, slapped up a little tape, and are planning to come back in the very near future for their official visit."

"Well," she smiled, "that's got to be kind of bad news for you, seeing as you've now slathered your fingerprints all over the joint."

I nodded. "If only I'd thought of all this before I went into the place."

"Still,"—her smile got bigger—"our boy Huyne, stickler or no, seems an understanding sort."

"That's one way to put it." My eyes opened up plenty. "And by the way, just exactly what did he want after I left?"

"Like he said, he just wanted to make sure I was all right." She stood in the doorway, not looking at me. "I think he was so stunned by your manly presence here that he skipped whatever else he might have wanted—for the time being."

"Good." I nodded. "I owe him one anyway for making me feel like a hound dog and for scaring poor little Joepye."

"You know you don't want to mess with that mean policeman."

"I don't know that at all." I squinted at her. "I just might want to mess with him a good bit."

"So." She disappeared again. "What's your next move then, cowboy?"

"Well, if there is a connection between Beth and Minnie, I'd like to know what it was."

"Maybe she just bought the photo somewhere."

"You didn't see the place, hon. This was not a well-thought-out decor. In fact, there wasn't anything else at all up in the bedroom. And in the living room there was a Domino's coupon sheet stuck up with a pushpin."

"I love that pizza."

"Be that as it may."

Silence.

Then, her face again in the doorframe. "By the way?"

"Yes?"

"I'm really glad you stayed the night last night. Just thought I'd mention it.

"Okay." I smiled. "It was worth it, actually, just to see the look on Huyne's face."

"Wish I'd been there." Back into the kitchen again.

"Man." I leaned forward. "I've really got to stop staying up all hours. I feel like a nap."

"A nap?" she called. "Some tough guy."

"How many times have I told you I never even *pretended* to be a tough guy?"

"Exactly seventeen thousand, I believe."

"And"—I finally managed to stand—"you still don't believe me."

"What are you doing?"

"Leaving," I told her, straightening my jacket.

"Before breakfast?" She made her grand appearance through the doorway with a brimming tray.

I stared. "You made breakfast for me?"

She gave me a curt nod. "Yes, sir, I did. It's a thank-you-Masked-Man breakfast, the kind the Lone Ranger would never stay and eat." Then she tossed her head toward the rarely used dining room table. "Sit."

Usually Dally's dining room table would be cluttered with newspapers and mail and half-read books. But it was cleared and spotless. Kind of frightening.

"Who came in and messed up your usual table decor?" I stood my ground.

"Move, wise guy." She shoved me a little with the tray.

We both sat; she shoved plates of food my way: French toast, smoked trout, red seedless grapes, bubble water, and more espresso.

I gave it all the once-over. "What's the occasion?"

She reached into her pants pocket and pulled out an envelope, "Payday." She dangled it for a moment, then laid it in front of me.

On the front it said "Dick test."

I looked up at her. "Test? Did I pass?"

She didn't smile. "A Dick test is the test doctors give you to see if you're immune to scarlet fever or not by injecting you with scarlet fever toxin."

"Really?"

"That's right." She nodded, staring at the envelope. "Take a look inside."

I did. It was full of hundred-dollar bills.

I looked up at her.

"As soon as Huyne left, some guy as big as a cement mixer came pounding on the door. Said the envelope was for you."

"Did he say who it was from?"

She leaned back in her chair. "The Pineapple."

"Oh."

"You haven't even started working on *his* case, have you?"

"Not exactly." I pulled the French toast toward me. "But it's been on my mind."

"So why do you think he sent you all this stuff about scarlet fever?"

"Well, you know about his penchant for hundred-dollar words and phrases." I put a fork in the toast. "It's my guess he's playing some kind of word game with me."

"Why?"

"Don't know. Just seems like his way."

"So what are you going to do about it—his Janey problem?"

"Don't know."

"Big money, mystery maladies, and Mickey Nichols—and you don't even have the courtesy to break a sweat." She leaned forward. "Are you just trying to make me irritated by being calm and obtuse?"

I paused a second in my attack on the fried bread. "When things threaten to get complicated and to overwhelm you, and there's a policeman, a gangster, a Joepye, a murderer, and a rich man all circling around you like hungry tigers, and you're eating a fine repast like this"—I looked up at her and took a bite—"all you can say is . . . 'Now *that's* a great breakfast.' "

"So you *are* trying to irritate me." She stared.

"Don't you know that Zen story?" I kept eating. "The guy hanging from a ledge with a vicious tiger above him and a hungry tiger down below? And what does he do? He reaches out, tastes a grape that's growing there on the cliff, and thinks, *Now that's a good grape.*" I smiled. "See?"

"I see that if Mickey 'the Pineapple' Nichols gets mad all over you," she insisted in a low voice, "you will be in one sad and sorry world, my very good friend, and in no condition to be eating grapes at all."

"Doing your Mickey imitation is not helping my digestion of this exceptional smoked trout. Where'd you get it?"

"Where I get my smoked trout is not the point."

"All right, I'll tell you the point." I set my fork down for emphasis. "The point is, I need to clear my mind, not clutter it. If I start worrying now about this-and-such riddle, or that-and-so threat, I can't do my job. Then I'm good for nothing."

"So you're trying to stay calm so you can get the job done."

"Right. No thanks to you, I might add." I picked up my fork again. "A lot of people mistake my relaxed grip on the situation for being lazy, you know."

"That's because," she began, already elevated in volume from the previous sentence, "you're always *saying* you're lazy."

"Correct." I nodded. "But I'm almost positive that you've figured it out by now: I'm deliberately trying to mislead everyone. It gives me an advantage to be incorrectly perceived, don't you think?"

"You don't think that I don't know by now that you'd like for me to *think* that it's just a pose when you say you're lazy but that you actually *are* lazy and you just *pretend* to be to cover that up?"

I looked up from my delicious breakfast. "I have no idea what that sentence even means."

"It means, don't play games with me, mister," she told me in no uncertain terms, shaking a finger dangerously close to my face, "because I know what you *really* are."

"Well, that's true." I smiled. "You might actually be the only person alive who knows what I really am." Smile got bigger. "I guess I'm lucky that way. Most people stagger around without anyone at all knowing who or what they are."

She took her time, but she gave me the big sigh. "Well, you sure can be sweet when you want to be."

"That?" I pushed my plate away. "I wasn't even trying with that."

"So maybe now you'll tell me," her voice was quieter again, "what you're going to do next."

I nodded, wiping my lips with the handy paper towel on the tray. "I'm going to visit Foggy Moskovitz."

She nearly lifted out of her chair. "Oh no you're not."

"I'm not?" I stuck a somewhat jaunty elbow on her table and leaned in. "And why not?"

"Because I don't want you anywhere near those thug types when your prints are peppered all over some murdered hooker's bedroom, that's why. You're liable to lose what good standing you have with Detective Huyne."

"And yet"—I forged bravely ahead—"Foggy is the key to Janey and Mickey." I cocked my head. "Hey. Mickey, Minnie, Foggy—is this a Disney movie?"

"You keep it up with the wisecracks. They love that sort of thing in prison."

"I'm not going to prison."

She stood up. "That's right, you're not, but no thanks to you." Big sigh. "I have to do everything."

I stood too. "*Everything* in this case means . . . ?"

"I'm going with you to visit Foggy. You need a shield."

From cruel experience I had long since realized the folly of denying Ms. Oglethorpe a trip if she really wanted to travel—and so we set off together for the wrong part of town.

14

THE ONE THAT
GOT AWAY

Of course, in Atlanta there are so many neighborhoods vying for that title that we could have gone
in nearly any direction. Southwest, where I'd spent
some of my younger days, could be pretty rough in a
juvenile delinquent sort of way. And for my money,
Buckhead's a bad environment just because of the
overabundance of young lawyers with hormones in
bars, but I digress.

In our particular case that day, we headed south
down Peachtree. After we passed through a stretch of
abandoned buildings and homeless nirvanas created
by belly-up businesses, we came to a stop just short of
the actual downtown area on a block that was domi-
nated—if that's not too coy a reference—by a huge
store called Good Vibrations, where they sold battery-

operated companionship and leather goods too expensive for your dog.

Foggy Moskovitz had an "office" in the lofts above the store, a small room with a few chairs, a coffee machine, and no windows.

Even though we hadn't called ahead, I was fairly certain he'd be there. He was known as a conscientious sort who, despite his reputation as a prime booster, had a work ethic that would shame a nineteenth-century farmer.

We parked on the side street at a broken meter and zipped up the stairs in back of the building.

His door was open, and there was soft humming coming from inside. I peered in, keeping Dally a little behind me, and there was Foggy, eyes closed, singing along to a tune he was listening to on his portable CD player. He was dressed in a gray double-breasted that could only be called dapper, cuff links, silk tie, hightone Italian loafers.

I knocked hard on the doorframe, and his eyes popped open.

"Huh?" He threw himself forward, put his hand over his heart like he was having an attack, but I knew what he was checking.

I put both hands out palms up. Look. No gun.

He smiled and sat back in his chair. He held up one finger, nodded, then punched the CD player.

"Mr. Tucker."

"Yes," I confirmed. "And look who's with me."

Dally poked her head in and smiled that smile.

He stood instantly. "Ms. Oglethorpe. My God."

He gave the room a quick once-over. "You must excuse the way the place looks. I am, as you can see, between decorators."

"Yes." She couldn't help laughing as she stepped in, "I can see that. Still, I love the simplicity of the current design."

"Universal essences"—he held up a finger again—"should not be unnecessarily multiplied."

"Occam's Razor." She nodded. "I'm familiar with the concept."

He stared at me. "Is she the finest woman in the Western Hemisphere?"

"Without a doubt," I told him in no uncertain terms.

"So to what may I owe the considerable pleasure of this visit?" He glanced between the two of us with just the right combination of amusement and suspicion.

I held out my palm again, this time to indicate the well-worn chairs. "Shall we take a seat?"

"Oh." He looked at the chairs. "I see. This is to be a sit-down visit."

"If you don't mind." I hesitated.

He took half a moment, then moved. "Who would mind?" And he stood holding the back of one of the chairs for a full twenty seconds before Dally realized he was holding it for her. Then he called out, "Daniel? Would you come in, please?"

Daniel Frank materialized in the doorway. He'd been behind us the whole time. I knew the guy from the old days, when we were both playing in bands. He was a tenor sax man, stood about four and a half feet tall, and was solid as a fire plug. He claimed to be related to Anne Frank, which I never believed, and to Leo Frank, which he had documented to my satisfaction one late, late night at Easy. Leo Frank was the man who had been incorrectly lynched—if that's not a redundancy—for the murder of Mary Phagan in the old days. Daniel had told me he still carried a grudge. The last time I'd seen him was when his band had played at a fund-raiser for Sam Massell, Atlanta's only Jewish mayor, which had been quite some time back.

"Flap." He nodded. "I thought that was you."

"Daniel. You know Ms. Oglethorpe?"

"Who doesn't?" He was still ready for trouble, in case trouble was paying a visit.

Dally just smiled and took the seat; the rest of us followed her lead.

"Mr. Moskovitz—" I began.

"Please. Foggy. We don't know each other that well?"

"I suppose we do." Even though we'd only met a few times before, I was willing to believe he was just that friendly a guy. "And in response to your kindness, I won't waste your time beating around the bush."

He liked that, you could see it on his face. He liked the respect it showed him. He was also quite enjoying his proximity to Ms. Oglethorpe—the envy, as he himself had previously established, of half the women in the world.

"If it's not too much trouble"—I didn't want to

risk undercutting our fine rapport by offending him now—"I'd like to ask you a few questions about our good friend Janey Finster."

Even thought there were no windows in the room, I knew a cloud had passed overhead. The light in the room actually seemed to change. Foggy's face lost some of its color. His voice, by the time he managed to find it again, had lost a little of its verve.

"Janey." That's all. But it was a lengthy dirge when he said it.

I waited for what I thought was the appropriate interval. "You're going to her memorial service?"

"No." He shook his head slowly. "I would prefer to remember Janey the way I saw her last."

I launched. "And would that have been New Year's Eve?"

His head shot up, and his eyes locked mine—but he didn't answer.

"You know," Dally rolled out casually, "Janey came over and spent a few nights with Flap after that incident."

"I know," he said slowly, still locked on my eyes.

Out of the corner of my eye, I could see Daniel tense up, ready for a sign from Foggy.

"I don't know what you're thinking." I didn't blink. "But if it has anything to do with taking out that gun you have inside your coat and popping me, or having Daniel do the same, let me just say that only night before last Mickey 'the Pineapple' Nichols tried the very same mode of communication. I will tell you what I told him. To wit: Go ahead and shoot. Bullets bounce off me. But this is a small room, and the ricochet might mess up the decor you've so carefully constructed or, God forbid, snag one of you or, even worse in my opinion, Ms. Oglethorpe here. We wouldn't want that."

He still stared. "No. We wouldn't want that. I have no inclination toward any such rudeness. I'm only wondering now if you might be here because you think I have something to do with Janey's murder. Daniel's also told me you've been overly friendly with a certain homicide detective recently."

I wasn't surprised. Daniel was known as a man who could find out the color of the socks you wore last Thursday if he really wanted to know.

I relaxed. "Well, Daniel certainly knows his stuff, as usual. But obviously you have something to do with Janey's murder. So do I. We knew her, we were among the last to see her, and the person who did the crime might be somebody we know. Ninety-three percent of all homicides in this man's city are committed by family or friends."

He nodded, relinquishing his gaze. "We're a friendly town all right."

"So can we talk about it?"

"I suppose so." His posture eased.

Daniel sat back.

The tension left Dally's face a little too, and we all shifted in our chairs.

"Janey was at your New Year's Eve party." I thought I might as well just jump right in.

"Yes."

"She was not invited."

"Oh." He disagreed. "She was plenty invited. It was Mickey I didn't particularly care to have there."

"You two do not see eye to eye."

"Unless"—he held up his famous, insistent finger—"it was where Janey was concerned. She was the apple of both sets of eyes, if I may use that phrase."

"You were sweet on Janey." Dally jumped in.

"Who wasn't?" He shrugged.

"So you were happy to see her at your party," she went on.

"Yes"—he wagged his head—"but I asked her to leave her gorilla outside. Which, may I say, did nothing to improve the aforementioned gorilla's disposition, and he was drunk anyway, so."

"He had been drinking Hot Tom and Jerry," I told Dally. "It's a fine old recipe."

"But to return to the topic," Foggy resumed, "Mick got worse as the night went on. I suppose I may have made it worse by dancing with Janey. Anyway, he eventually took a swing at me, as I am sure you have heard. Only I am fast and moved out of the way. This unfortunately was bad news for Jane—"

"Who got clipped by Mickey's wide swing—" I let Dally know.

"And she got madder than I've ever seen her," Foggy finished.

"So you left the party—your own party—with her." I just wanted to confirm the facts.

"She wanted to get out," he told me. "Who wouldn't? I am nothing if not a gentleman. I offered her a ride home. She didn't want to go home. She wanted to go somewhere Mickey could not find her, in his condition. I offered my place, but she wisely concluded that a thing of that sort would only make matters worse in the event Mick should find us. So it was decided that we roll on over to your pad."

Dally shot me a glance. "That was . . . what, the third time she'd come over to your place like that?"

"I think," I told her. "Mickey never seemed to guess where she was when she was with me."

"And she only stayed that night?" Dally said, mostly to see what Foggy's reaction was, I guess. She knew Janey had stayed the next night too.

"No," I played along, "she went back home with some of her girlfriends and got a few things, then came back and spent the next night with me too. Said it took Mickey a day to sober up and another to calm down. She went home after sundown on the night of the second."

"And she was found dead in her bed on the fourth," Dally gave out, a little chillier than I thought necessary.

But it had an effect.

"Why didn't she just come home with me?" Foggy said, leaning forward and rubbing his face with his hands. "Or even stay with you?" He pointed my way without looking.

"So after your party, you never saw her again?" Dally was pressing pretty hard.

"She called me."

"She did?" I sat forward. "When?"

"From your place. On the second." He looked up again. "She was thinking about throwing Mickey over, I believe, because she kept asking me a lot of cute questions. Like did I ever think about going legit and would it kill me to have a better office—that kind of thing. You know, teasing."

"And that was it?" I pressed.

"I tried calling her at her place the next day, but it was no good. I got the machine. I hate to think that she could have been lying there—"

But I broke in. "Absolutely no point in dwelling on that."

He stopped; then he nodded. "You're right. Isn't it amusing the way the human mind seems to find ways of torturing itself?"

Foggy's face seemed to betray a territory in his mind where ghosts and regrets played tag.

"Very amusing," I agreed, "but more to the point, the police have arrested Mickey for Janey's murder."

"Yes." He pinched his lips. "I had also heard this from Daniel."

"I think they have the wrong guy," I kept on. "I know Mick's reputation, but anybody with half an eye could see he was crazy over the kid."

"Love will, however, make a man do strange things." He sat up a little.

"I was trying to explain that to Mickey just the other night—and, in fact, concerning the very same woman."

"For example," he went right on, "I was actually thinking of going legit—for Jane. How about *that*?"

"But you've decided against that now?" Dally pitched in.

"Yes," he nodded. "A man must follow his heart."

"And your heart is in petty theft?" She shook her head.

"Not exactly. But I enjoy the idea of being outside the rules, free from the ordinary confines of the normal man's life." He looked between Dally and me. "Much like the two of you, I would imagine."

"I'll skip the touché" I nodded, "and go right for the big question: You *do* think Mickey popped Janey?"

He enumerated. "One, Janey did not have an enemy in this world; two, ninety-three percent of all homicides in Atlanta are perpetrated by someone who knows the victim intimately, as you just said; and C, Mickey is quite rightly notorious for his ways. He's the one who did those two topless dancers that got stuck in the trunk of a Buick a while back. Remember that one?"

I glanced at Dally again, smiling. "Yeah, I remember that one, and I happen to know your theory is way off. But this is the way a legend grows, I guess. A person builds his reputation on innuendo and bravado, see?"

"Example?" Daniel wanted to know. He seemed to have a genuine interest in the concept, a professional interest.

"When's the last time," I obliged, "that anyone in Atlanta—since we all seem to be up on the latest crime statistics—was actually killed by a hand grenade? Would you happen to know?"

Daniel smiled and shook his head. "You've got me."

"That bit of homicidal esoterica has eluded me as well." Foggy raised his eyebrows.

"Well," I allowed, "the fact is, there is not a single case on record at the police department in the last twenty years. Now I have heard at least five stories about guys Mickey blew up just this past few months. But I have come to believe that they are just that: stories. You get my drift."

"I believe," Foggy smiled, "that what you have there is more a *current* than a simple *drift,* but I get it nevertheless. You wish me to believe that Mick is harmless—a tough sell for me, because, you see, he once played a game of sidewalk basketball with my head. Bounced me silly. I still have the occasional lapse of memory. I believe he did permanent damage. So, you see, it is my belief that he is a menace, a misogynist, and a mook. And it would be perfectly fine by me if he rotted in the jug like a dead *fish.* I hope I make myself clear!"

Silence.

Daniel smiled quietly. "Well, Ms. Oglethorpe, how are things down at the club?"

She took a second to adjust to the question, then smiled as only she can. "Thank you for asking, Daniel. Business is good; music's better than ever."

"I like Gwen Hughes. She's playing this week, I believe?"

"Come on down," she nodded. "Flap will treat you to some of his private stock."

He knew what she meant. "That French red's not for me." He shook his head. "I'll have a scotch, straight, no chaser—"

"In honor of the great Thelonius Monk." I picked up the mood.

"Yes." Daniel nodded. " 'Straight, No Chaser.' Great tune."

Our little small talk had given Foggy a chance to catch his breath and relax his shoulders.

"You're a good friend, Daniel." That's all he said.

Daniel's smile only grew warmer.

"Just one or two more questions," I jumped back in, "about your party that night, your New Year's Eve party; then we'll be out of your hair."

Foggy nodded.

"Good. I'll once again get right to the point. Do you know a little guy named Joepye Adder?"

"The park guy? The nut? Yeah, I know who he is."

"Joepye." Daniel looked at Dally. "Isn't that a weed?"

"It's got a pretty flower in the summer, though," I nodded, then back at Foggy: "Was he at your party?"

"Joepye." He squinted. "Not by invitation."

"Right, but Mickey wasn't exactly an invited guest either."

"Granted."

"So maybe Joe and some kid who might have looked a little like Janey—by the name of Beth Dane, who was, incidentally, the niece of Irgo Dane"—

"The musician?" He cocked his head.

I nodded curtly. "That was his niece that got iced in the park just the other night. I assume you've heard all about that?"

"And I wish I hadn't." He closed his eyes a moment. It really gave the impression he was saying a quick prayer, but maybe he was just taking his time blinking. "That was his niece?"

"Mr. Dane," Daniel interjected out of the blue. "What a strange one he is."

"Strange?" I looked at him.

"I'm told his predilections tend toward the unusual, yes." He shook his head and was about to say more, but he was interrupted.

"One point at a time." A look from Mr. Moskovitz silenced Daniel. "You were saying," Foggy went on, "that his niece was at my New Year's Eve party."

"That's what I'm getting at." I went right on. "They may have crashed your party, this odd couple. And it might be the last time we ever saw her alive too—the niece."

"What a town this is." He stared far off, thinking. Then: "You know, when you play host to a big affair of that sort, you don't really have the complete attention to detail, or I mean, I don't. I'm more the general and gregarious type at a party, and so a few things could slip by me."

"Agreed." I nodded.

"Still, it does not mean that they were not there." He nodded. "Daniel? Would you mind doing a little checking?"

Daniel gave a curt nod.

"But not for Mickey." Foggy wanted to make it clear to me. "I will look into this simply because you asked nicely."

"No"—I stood slowly—"you will look into this because you'd like to know who really killed Janey just as bad as the rest of us would."

"Okay." He nodded, standing too. "Maybe even worse, because she's the one that got away, Flap." Then he looked at the floor. His voice took a dive again, and he spoke very slowly. "And when you are dead, I believe you have most likely gotten away for good."

15

MEN IN BLUE

"Well, thank you both for checking on Joepye and Beth Dane." I didn't know what else to say. "And thank you for your very informative commentary. Daniel, good to see you."

Daniel stood formally. "Yes, Flap. We should catch up."

"You think I don't know." Foggy's voice gained in strength again. He stared up at me. "But I know. You didn't come here just to meet with me today. You came to set a wheel in motion, this wheel of inquiry and doubt. You hope it will flush something out. What that *something* is, I have no idea. But I will still have Daniel ask around—because I also want to know, as you were saying."

"Mr. Moskovitz"—I stood, offered Dally my arm—"you are as perceptive as you are convivial, and I admire intelligence in a man who has such terrible taste in office decor."

He smiled and finally stood along with the rest of us. "And I admire a man who can say such a thing and not make anybody mad."

I pushed open the door and looked down the stairs. The parking lot was swarming with men in blue.

"Hey." I stopped at the top of the stairs. "There must be a hundred cops downstairs."

"Oh." Daniel rubbed his eyes. "That's my fault. I nearly forgot. I called them when you were coming up the back stairs. I had no idea what you wanted. I thought it might create a diversion, just in case we needed one. I told them that I worked here and I was calling in a complaint about illegal sexual goings-on in the establishment downstairs. Five will get you ten I was right. There's always something bad going on in there."

I stared at him. "You heard us coming? And you called up a diversion?"

He nodded.

I turned to Foggy. "So, your surprise when I came to your door—"

"Was an act." Foggy smiled. "I am very much more than you think I am, my friend."

I ignored that and stared down at the policemen in the parking lot. "How was this going to help you?"

"Would you mess with me knowing there were a hundred cops down there," Foggy said simply, "this door being your only way out?"

"Good point."

Dally spoke up. "By the way, Foggy?"

"Yes?"

"You wouldn't know—you or Daniel—anything about scarlet fever, would you?"

We all stared at Dally for almost a full minute while the policemen in the parking lot began to quiet down.

"Now, it's a funny thing you should ask me that." Foggy went and closed the door himself.

"Really?" Dally watched him carefully. "How is it funny, exactly?"

"Well," he began, "it is funny primarily because Daniel tells me that a certain quantity of scarlet fever gunk, or whatever you would call it, has been discussed in the lower circles of our . . . acquaintances."

"Scarlet fever *what*?" I beat Dally to the question.

"Stuff. What they give you to find out if you're immune to the disease, am I right?" He turned to Daniel.

"Something like that." Daniel nodded.

"Somebody stole it?" Dally jumped in. "By your acquaintances, you mean like fences?"

"Who the hell would steal that?" I stared at Dally.

"Not just that." Daniel chimed in. "The party in question stole all manner of germs or diseases, as far as we can tell—from some medical testing facility over at the CDC."

Foggy looked back and forth between all of us. "Some world, huh?"

"Who would *buy* that kind of thing?" I still hadn't managed to hide my incredulity.

"Oh, it's been my experience," Foggy spoke softly, "that anything you can steal, somebody else would want to buy. Why that is, I have no idea. But this is human nature."

Dally shouldn't have, but she spoke out right in front of Foggy. "What's it got to do with Mickey Nichols?"

I looked at the two men, as if they actually might have the answer.

Foggy gave me, instead, the big shrug. "Much as I hate to let the guy off the hook on any score, we have *not* heard anything about Mick being involved in this particular endeavor. He might have heard something, same as me—he's got quite an information syndicate, even in the jug, I'd imagine. But as far as his being connected to this? That's not what we heard."

"Could you tell us"—I thought I'd give it a shot— "what you *did* hear?"

"I already did. I don't know anything more. Daniel?" He turned.

"Sorry," Daniel said quietly. "I wish I could help."

I smiled at him. "You already helped enough. You gave me more to worry about . . . and you called the cops on me. Quit helping."

"If you say so." Daniel smiled. We both knew his help was just beginning.

In the parking lot the cops gave Dally and me a suspicious look, but they had seen us leave from upstairs, a perfectly respectable business establishment called, I had just noticed, Imports of the World. There was even a nice plastic sign over the door.

So, except for the general discomfort of having policemen stare at our every move, the walk to the car and the drive away occurred silently and without event.

But as soon as we were down the block, Dally let out a big "Well."

"Well, indeed." I had to agree. "That was certainly *some* information we got."

"Thanks mostly to me, at least about the toxins or whatever they are.'

"Right." I smiled at her. "Thanks."

"Don't mention it," she shot right back.

"Look, if you don't mind, I'd like to drop you off and do the rest of my rounds solo. Don't you have work to do or a club to run or something?"

"Sort of," she hedged. "I don't like the idea of being by myself, if you must know." She stared out the window. "I really . . . liked Minnie."

I didn't know what to say to that, so I just kept my mouth shut. This is what I've learned from long experience with the finest woman in the Western Hemisphere: Sometimes you just have to shut up and listen.

That's all you have to do to help. You don't have to always be the Lone Ranger, riding in to fix it all and then skidding away without so much as a "Thank you, Masked Man." Sometimes all you have to be is *there*.

It paid off. She didn't look at me, but she went on talking. "She used to come down sometimes when I was getting home. You know, like, four or five in the morning sometimes. She'd have been up working in her darkroom and lost track of the time. I admired that. I admire anyone who can get that lost in their art or their work. Plus, her art was swell." Finally turning to me: "You know, I'd really like to know how one of her photos got into that kid's apartment you just saw—if it really was one of hers."

"It's one of the things I'll be checking." I nodded. "But at the moment I'd like to know a little bit more about stolen toxins too. Especially since Mick seems to have suggested it has something to do with scarlet fever."

"So let me go with you."

I began to be visited by all the creepy images of people hanging from lampposts and faces bloated from strangulation I'd seen over the past fifty hours or so. It occurred to me then that a little company—not to mention somebody to talk to when it got weird again—wouldn't be such a bad thing.

"Okay," I nodded, "but on one condition."

"What is it?"

"I'll let you go with me"—I shrugged—"if you let

me go with you too. That way nobody's just along for the ride."

She looked back out the window. "If you weren't already my favorite boy," she said so softly that I almost didn't hear, "you would be now."

16

GERM TOWN

The Centers for Disease Control are over by Emory University, and they're a fair-size complex. Some people don't like living near the CDC, especially when there's talk in the local papers of the kind of samples they get through the mail.

I happened to have a friend, this guy Paul, who sometimes did research for the CDC. He worked at Georgia Tech mostly, but he was one Renaissance biologist. It being a Tuesday, he would ordinarily be in his little lab at the Centers. So I nosed the car in his direction, up Piedmont, out Ponce, left at Fernbank.

Twenty minutes later the front desk was paging him to come out and greet his "luncheon appointment," as we had described ourselves.

Of course he had no idea who was waiting for him,

but when he saw Dally and me in the lobby, he picked up his step. He was always happy to see Dally.

"Hey!" He waved. "I was just thinking about you."

"Save it, Paul, we're here on business." I gave him the stern look.

"Oh." He slowed. "Business. Okay, come on back."

I moved closer to him. "In the interest of time, let me just tell you why we're here."

"You're working on the thing with the girls hanging in Piedmont Park." He nodded sagely.

"What makes you think that?"

"Please." He pulled his head back from me a little and gave me something of an attitudinal look. "Who else would be working on such a weird deal?"

"Okay, you've guessed correctly, but that's not exactly why I'm here."

"Oh?"

We rounded a corner, and he waved at some beefy security goon so we could all go into a small lab.

Dally stared backward. "Those security guys are always there?"

He nodded. "Day and night."

I lowered my voice. "So then how did somebody just recently steal a whole bunch of toxic poison stuff from here?"

"Shh!" He flinched like I'd jabbed him and lowered his voice to a whisper. "You can't just talk about that here. It's a very sensitive issue."

"I'd imagine." I stared around the little room "So what got stolen exactly?"

"What makes you think I'd know?" He didn't even ask how I'd know about such a thing. Paul just accepted that I found things out.

"Please." I gave him back the very same look he'd given me only an instant before. "Like anybody else would know more about such a weird deal."

"Funny." He nodded, but he wasn't smiling. "See, this is bad. I think the guys who stole it don't know what they've got. It seemed like a pretty inept job to me. No prints, but a lot of hair and fiber and other stuff. And a lot of handling the cases we had our samples in. Anybody who'd really known what we had in there would have been a ton more careful."

"A ton?" Dally's whisper matched Paul's.

"Usually a pro who's snatching something like that will suit up like it's Hiroshima. Whoever grabbed this lot just strolled in and picked up the first case marked 'Toxic.' That's what I think."

"It was just lying around in the open?" Looking around at all the locked cabinets, I couldn't believe that. "And wasn't the alleged perpetrator seen on those security cameras?" I pointed to the one in the corner of our very room.

Paul looked at us both. "We're not supposed to talk about this, okay?" Then he lowered his voice even more. I could barely hear him.

"Somebody jammed the cameras for, like, ten minutes, apparently—plugged something into the electrical system from outside the building, if you can believe that. There was a commotion outside at the same time, the guards took a look, the thief was in here for five of those minutes. A cabinet marked 'Toxic', that one there"—he pointed—"was popped open, and one case was taken. I think it was kids, maybe looking to get some kind of weird high, or maybe some creep looking for an untraceable murder weapon. But amateurs, I'm positive of that."

I stared. "Amateurs? It's that easy to break into this place, with all the germs and biological warfare you've got lying around here?"

"Well, if we're working on some big anthrax deal"—Paul stared back, irritated—"we're a little more careful, but this is routine gunk we're dealing with, Flap."

Dally glanced around the room. "So what *was* in the case?"

"Scarlet fever, rabies, and some kind of spider venom."

"Why do you even have that kind of thing here at the moment?" I asked him. "Or is it always just lying around handy?"

"Well," he sighed, collecting his thoughts, "there's some kind of outbreak of scarlet fever in a little rural part of Argentina; we're helping with that. We're looking for an even quicker way of getting somebody over rabies, so we had that here in this lab too. And the spider venom is for some kind of allergy/immune system research that I didn't have anything to do with."

Dally squinted. "Why were all three in the same case? Some kind of sampler?"

"Actually"—his voice began to rise to a normal level again—"we were about to send that case out, along with some of the research, to another facility in Boston for verification of our findings."

"That case was about to be mailed out?" I let my voice rise too. "You just send this through the *mail*?"

"Of course you have to have a special notification." He nodded. "It has to be marked and shipped carefully. And some hell-special container. I'm telling you, Flap, you could set off an atom bomb next to these things and they still wouldn't break open. It's safe."

"Okay," I nodded. "Okay."

Suddenly I was feeling a little dizzy.

Dally stared at me, concerned. "Flap?"

"What's that smell in here?"

Paul looked around. "Smell? I don't notice any smell."

"Jesus." I could hardly breathe. "I think there must be something in here I'm allergic to, or something. I've got to get some air."

Paul sniffed. "Smells like it always does."

"Is it just the smell?" Dally took a step my way.

"Well," I admitted, "you know how I told you I was going to keep my mind open, keep myself clear of all this clutter?"

"Yes." She moved a little closer.

"I lied. It's all crammed in my brain now, and it's just about to bust my head wide open."

Paul nodded. "Well, get out of here then. I don't want to see that—brain guts all over the place."

I stared. "And you call yourself a man of science."

But Dally was wise. "You'd like to get back to your place."

I knew what she was getting at. "Yes, I would."

"I understand. You're probably just tired."

We started out before Paul realized we were leaving.

"Oh"—he suddenly lurched forward—"let met get the door. Damn. Short visit. Come back when you can't stay so long, like they say."

We were down the hall and out into the cold air before we said another word. Dally waved good-bye to Paul.

We settled into the car. Dally wanted to drive. Okay by me.

"I'm better now. I was just momentary overloaded. And that room had a funny smell."

"Probably the formaldehyde," she said. "I hate it."

I looked out the window.

"You're taking me back home?"

"Don't you want to go back home? Isn't it time for you to do . . . you know . . . the *thing*?"

I slumped down in the car seat, "let's not talk about *that* again."

17

BAD DAY IN
DREAMLAND

Ordinarily twilight is my favorite part of the day, because the day's work is done and a glass or two of red wine would be in order. But that particular Tuesday night was different.

I'd spent most of the afternoon trying to trick myself into dreamland. But the dream was elusive, and the second half of the day had been wasted. I just couldn't make the trick work.

"The trick" is only a way of getting ahold of the big picture, really. Most people wander around all day seeing things but not realizing what they've seen, hearing things but not letting those things register. My little gimmick is a way of putting all those unregistered bits and pieces together so that they make the big picture.

I sit and clear my mind of everything, if I can manage it, and images come and assemble themselves on the blank canvas, and I know more than I did before. A lot of people will try to tell you it's something otherworldly, like a magic spell. But that attitude just confuses the process for me, ultimately.

What I do, when I do it right, is just an unexplored portion of ordinary reality. We only see certain wavelengths of light, for example, but that doesn't mean all the other wavelengths aren't there—or that they *are* there but consist of something mysterious or mystical. It's just that we can't see them at a certain moment. I mean, you know, I can't see Wyoming from my apartment, but my belief that it's out there somewhere is hardly spiritual. It's not even something you have to accept on faith. It's just a bit of information that most of us accept without even thinking about it at all. Well, my little trick is just another bit of Wyoming that most people can't see from where they live, but it's there just the same, take my word for it.

Only that particular Tuesday, it wasn't there at all.

So what could I do but pick up the phone and call Dally?

"Hello?" She sounded mad.

"Hey." I tried to sound neutral. "What's the matter?"

"No," she said coolly, "I'm happy with my current long-distance carrier, thank you."

"You've got company."

"Yes." She sounded harder. "But I don't need expanded service."

"Cops?"

"Right again," she was really worked up. "But my *no* is final. Please don't call here again today."

"You don't want me over there?"

"That's correct." Her mouth must have moved away from the telephone because her voice sounded a little muffled; she was looking at someone else in the room. "I don't."

"Trouble?"

"Yes. Good-bye." And she hung up.

Well. That is what they often call "a fine how-do-you-do." I was in need of some serious consolation, and the only person I wanted it from was in some kind of trouble that she didn't want me helping with. What to do?

Here's a secret. When you spend all afternoon trying to do something that just won't get done, action really helps. Sometimes you just have to get out and do something. Any action at all is better than doing nothing. Get up. Get out. To be is to do.

So in a way I was glad of the distraction. I roused myself with a fair amount of speed and got my car to the end of her block within seven minutes. The sun was going down, and the quality of light was strange and hazy, a little golden.

Out front of her place there were two squad cars and an unmarked sedan that looked very much like the one that belonged to Detective Huyne.

What could make such a scene?

The top lights weren't spinning, so this was more of a visit than, say, a raid. Still: three carloads. And she didn't want me anywhere near the place; that was clear from her tone alone.

It came to me that perhaps our detective friend might have imagined I'd still be at Dally's house, and all the fuss was over me. Maybe Foggy said something he ought not to have said. Maybe Mickey let something out of the bag that made Huyne suspicious of me. Maybe Joepye had come up with more new theories about the dead girls.

A regrettable but undeniable urge in the direction of the better part of valor forced me off the sidewalk and back into my car. Then it occurred to me that I had been presented with the perfect time to visit Mickey in the lockup with a degree of privacy, since it was certain, at least, that Huyne wasn't at the station house.

I didn't turn my lights on. I backed up very slowly, turned around on the one-way street in the next block, and headed for downtown.

18

MICKEY'S MONKEY

Traffic was a dream that time of the evening, and I hit Mickey's postdinner visiting hour almost perfectly.

With a minimum of rigmarole, mostly because of my aforementioned pal Detective Winston, I got in to see him.

"Flap Tucker." Mickey was calm. "What news?"

I looked him right in the eye. "What's the idea of sending me a thousand-dollar retainer and a two-dollar clue?"

"What do you mean?" But there was no surprise or resistance in his voice. He just wanted me to ask the right questions.

"Well," I began, "I got the hint. In fact, three samples of some pretty potent microbes were stolen just recently from a lab at the CDC, including scarlet fever toxin."

"As I had heard," he intoned, like some Damon Runyon Buddha.

"Well, (A) how did you know? And (B) so what?"

"How I knew is my remarkable syndicate of information. You should really try, Flap, to get into the twentieth century before it is all over but the shouting, and buy yourself a computer. The Internet is to our intellectual life what the Universal Unconscious is to our psychological life. In fact, the Internet *is* the new Universal Unconscious. It's not even a *metaphor* anymore."

Though I never ceased to be surprised at his erudition, I forged foolishly ahead with my line of inquiry. "And what about the 'so what' portion of the program?"

"They say Janey was smothered to death."

"They do." I nodded.

"And they say my prints were all over the joint when they found her."

"Correct."

He looked down for a second and faltered. "That's because I was there. It was my prints, Flap."

"Okay."

"They will not take me seriously, but here is the story: I came over to her place to apologize on the night of January second"—he was cranking it out like he'd told a hundred times, which he probably had, at that point—"and I found her body. She had asphyxiated, I believe. There were no marks, no struggle. She was laid out . . . like an angel. I couldn't bear to see her eyes like that, all bugged out—and her face blue . . . so I grabbed the pillow and put it over her."

I stared. "In the first place, the cops aren't that stupid. They know the difference between poisoning—which I assume is what you're getting at—and suffocation by pillow."

He stared right back. "You and I know Janey as a sweet kid who maybe shouldn't have hung out with types like us. The cops think of her as *one of us,* wouldn't you say?"

"Could be right." I nodded slowly. I was thinking of how quickly Dane's niece had become a so-called suicide, which was much more farfetched than what Mick was telling me.

"So before I could even work my magic connections and get somebody to perform an autopsy, Janey's body is shuffled off to the crematorium, and all that's left is something to scatter on the roses in the park."

"She's already been cremated? That seems kind of . . . fast."

"Exactly. And the memorial ceremony's tomorrow." He looked down again. "I can't stop thinking about her, Flap. It's like, as they used to say in the old gangster films, I have that well-known monkey on my back. I can't stop thinking."

"I know what a problem that can be." I rubbed my

eyes for a second. "But what makes you think there's any link at all between the stolen toxins and this business?"

"Well"—he started slowly, gathering his strength again, with what could only have been described as an *atomic* twinkle in his eye, "maybe it's because the private notes of one Detective Burnish Huyne would indicate that he suspects exactly the same thing."

"Okay, in the first place, how would you know something like that?" I shook my head. "I'm positive Detective Huyne does not post his notes on the Net."

He shrugged. "A guy distracts him while he's writing his reports. Some other guy looks over his shoulder. Picking his mind is simpler than picking his pocket. Simplicity itself."

"Somebody you know looked over his shoulder while he was writing his notes? How twentieth century is that?" I had to smile. "But you are something of a Machiavellian wonder, if I may use that term."

"Use away." He smiled back brightly. "I love that term. I always appreciate it when you try to match my level of grammatical prowess."

"Still," I hesitated, "there are only about a thousand holes in the theory."

"That may be," he nodded. "But why does Huyne have that theory in the first place? That's what we want to find out, wouldn't you think?"

I stood. "Possibly." I cleared my throat. "I don't suppose they're letting you out to go to Janey's service tomorrow."

"No." He was trying to the stoic version of tough: His mouth was set hard, but his eyes gave him away.

"How about if I go, then," I told him, "and say good-bye for you."

He tried to answer, but he didn't manage it.

19

A BIGGER BITE

For some reason I found the idea of calling Dally's house from the downtown police station amusing, so I dialed her up on one of the pay phones.

"Hello?" She was her old self again.

"So," I spoke smoothly into the receiver, "care for dinner?"

"Hey." She was glad to hear my voice, I could tell. "I have to tell you I'm relieved that you didn't mess around and come over here when you called before—"

"Because Huyne and a gaggle of investigators were at the time paying you a visit. I know. I did come over. But when I saw the cars, I beat it. I've been talking to Mickey instead."

"Oh, really."

"Yes, really. So, dinner?"

"You'll pick me up? I have so much to tell you from my recent visitation."

"Right," I told her, "so let's just go on over to Le Giverny."

"Oh." She sounded surprised, impressed.

"I've got an envelope filled with dinner money, remember. And I haven't tried the new snails they have on the menu yet."

"Plus," she picked right up, "they put the '86 Simard on the wine list."

"At a remarkable inflated price."

"What do you care? You've got an envelope." That smile. "So how was your Tao session today, tell me?"

"On the fritz."

"What?"

"Didn't happen." I tried not to sound too dejected. "I think it's broken."

"You think your Tao's broken?"

"Somehow." I shifted the phone. "Maybe."

"Well"—she spoke quickly, in something of a mocking tone, I thought—"then we don't have a moment to lose. Get over here fast. We've got to get some snails and overpriced wine into you before the hour's out."

Big grin from me. "I'm for that."

Le Giverny's a small place, but we were early enough on a weeknight to manage a table. It was noisy and full and smelled like a bistro in Paris.

"I'll go first," Dally announced, just as she finished

pouring my second glass of Simard. "Huyne and his pals were visiting me because one of the gentlemen in the parking lot down from Foggy's Imports happened to recognize me as we made it to your car."

"You really are the policeman's friend these days."

"Shut up." She smiled sweetly. "They also knew you. Huyne thought you'd be with me, and he wanted to haul us both in, along with Foggy—who is nowhere to be found, by the way—and even our boy Paul."

"They even wanted to haul in Paul? Huyne has been keeping an eye on us then."

"Wouldn't you have noticed a tail?"

"Usually." I nodded. "But something's not right about all this. I'm really off-kilter, or something. Maybe it's just the two cases at the same time and a little overly personal involvement."

"Personal?" I thought I might have sensed a little jealousy in the air.

"Not like what you're thinking." I smiled. "But let's take a quick check of the facts: I knew the kid who got smothered—if that's how she died at all, but that's another story I'll tell you in a second. I know Dane, and he knows me. I've known Joepye for years, and he's telling the cops I might have iced the girls all the while he's taking me to see both of them before the cops get there. And on top of it all, I got shot at in my own club?"

"Whose club?"

"Don't I remember"—I looked down at my glass—"something about a silent partner paper thing involving me in your unsavory establishment?"

"So you got shot at." Big shrug, avoiding that particular issue. "Like that hasn't happened before."

I stared off. "I've got a weird feeling in my head." I got lost momentarily in that feeling. "What if Mickey actually shot me that night, I'm lying in a hospital bed, and this is all an opiated hallucination? Or what if he really did kill me, and I just don't know I'm dead yet, still wondering around like a Chinese ghost in one of those stories I'm all the time reading?" Healthy sip of wine. "Ever feel completely abstracted like that?"

"What the hell is the matter with you?" She leaned forward impatiently. "You don't have time for this kind of goofy meandering. I mean, it's fine for you when there's nothing else to do, but at the moment you've got to stay on the beam, Mr. Tucker, and cut out all that metaphysical onanism."

I came out of my mood pretty quickly. "Hey. Nice turn of the phrase." I caught her eye. "And thanks." Sip of wine. "What in fact *is* the matter with me?"

"You look okay." She started hesitantly. "Except you look like you could use a little extra shut-eye."

"What?"

"Dark circles, is all."

"Ah, well, I've been up the past few nights." I nodded, hefting my wineglass again. "So let me tell you what Mickey told me."

"Right. Good." It was obvious that she was happy to get me out of the weird zone and back on track.

"He tells me that Detective Huyne suspects a connection between the toxins Paul told us about and the murders of the hanging girls. He pickpocketed the guy's mind."

"What?"

"Nothing," I smiled, "he just got a glance at the detective's private notes. Also, get this: Mick was in fact at the murder scene, at Janey's. He found her dead, touched everything in sight so as to get his fingerprints all over everything, and then split."

"And he's not nearly that stupid." She lifted her glass.

"Exactly. Or that calm, remember. He's supposed to be the violent type, not the snuff-them-in-their-sleep type."

Our snails came. An odd recipe: They were wood-smoked and without a hint of garlic or butter.

"Where does this leave us with the police, by the way?" I asked Dally before I popped the first one in my mouth. "Are they looking for me? Am I, by any chance, illegally at large?"

"Well"—she didn't wait, took a bite in mid-sentence—"remember your information exchange agreement with Huyne? Hey, these snails are great."

"Yeah," I agreed, "the normal way always has too much butter for me. And yes, I remember my agreement with the detective."

"Anyway," she went on, "I think you're okay for the time being. I told him everything: what we got from Foggy and from Paul. That satisfied his information exchange quotient for the day, and he left."

"Because he's got a crush on you the size of Wyoming. He wouldn't have gone away that easily otherwise, do you think?"

"Wyoming?"

"Sorry"—I shrugged—"that's from some thinking a little earlier in my day. While I was sitting around *not* doing my thing."

"So, your thing's got engine trouble or something?" She'd already finished her snails.

"I don't know what it is." I got my last snail taken care of quickly, because I saw her eyeing it. "But I had absolutely no luck today. And I'm telling you, it's left me a little droopy."

"A little *what*?"

"I'm tired, is all—like you said."

"Maybe it's just like *you* said." She shrugged. "Sensory overload. You've got a lot to think about."

"I guess."

Our salads came, and we spent the next fifteen or twenty talking about how good it was, how to duplicate various recipes in our own little kitchens—anything to avoid the real issue. I had never had trouble with my trick before, and I guess it scared us both a little. Maybe it was that I hadn't used it in a while. Maybe I'd used it all up.

I mean, what if it was gone forever? That's what I was thinking. What if I could never see the big picture again? What if all I could do was wander around in this life looking at the trees and never again seeing the forest? I'd miss the forest. I liked the forest. It's, as they say, lovely, dark, and deep.

Dally's the one who finally met the issue head-on, God bless her.

"So, okay, how about if it's like riding on a horse. How about if you just get back in there and try it again after dinner?"

"No good." I shook my head. "I've already had this very nice wine and you can't do the thing with a fuzzy head."

"Like your head's not fuzzy *all* the time."

"There's no doing it tonight." I was firm on that. "The angel won't kiss you if you've had too much to drink, and tonight it's my plan to have too much. But first thing in the morning."

She nodded slowly, and our meals came. I had the trout in parchment and she had her perennial Pasta Monet. All was well and relatively silent for the next half hour.

When she finally laid down her fork, sipped the last of the wine in her glass, and leaned forward to look at the dessert menu, she had made up her mind: "You're staying with me again tonight. (A) I want the company. (B) I'll see to it that the first thing you do in the morning is get down to business with your little concentration exercises. (C) It'll confuse Detective Huyne, who, I am convinced, will be back to visit me tomorrow."

I smiled. "Reason number C is by far the most compelling." I rapped the table. "I'll do it."

She had a B&B, I had a cognac; we paid with some of the cash from my magic envelope and split.

In the parking lot Dally looked up at the stars in

the cold January air. "You know, some of those things are actually all gone—those stars. Burned out. The only reason we still think we see them is just that the light hasn't finished making it all the way to our little corner."

"Yeah." I looked at her sideways. "I know."

"So, we're looking at the past when we look up at the sky."

"Okay." I nodded slowly, wondering where she was going.

"So the sky we're seeing now? It's not accurate. It's a lie."

"Dally?"

She finally turned to look at me. "The *big picture* that you're always going on about? The one you have to get a glimpse of to get yourself organized around your so-called cases? It's like the sky. It's no more definitive than all the little pictures. It's just a bigger bite of the illusion."

I just stared at the curve of her cheek as she turned her face back up to the stars.

20

CLATTER

Maybe it was the good night's rest—I'd slept like the dead—or the hot shower. Maybe it was the calm air in the house; Dally had tidied up her living room. Or, most likely, it was the forty-five minutes I'd spent considering how absolutely correct our Ms. Oglethorpe had been about the nighttime sky. What I was so desperate to get ahold of—the big picture, the prize behind the golden curtain—was just another trick of light, a lie of the mind, a gander at the grand illusion.

So, with the pressure off, as it were, I had slipped more easily than I ever would have imagined the day before, right into a state of extreme relaxation. I was letting images float into and out of my field of vision as if I were watching fish swimming in a clear pond.

All you have to do really is breathe. If all you are is

breath, the rest comes easy. In. Out. Nothing to it. Just sit, and the angel creeps up behind you and kisses you with light.

There was the hazy golden glow in front of my eyes. There were bright fish swimming.

Janey's face. Beth Dane's face. Old man Dane playing a familiar tune on his bass—which looked like a naked woman from the back—with a hacksaw. Joepye picking my pocket. Girls in a long line dancing the tango. Spiders crawling on a corpse. Beth hanging in one of Minnie's photographs. Joepye being arrested over and over again. Mickey shooting me in the heart.

I felt the bullet inside me, but all the tissue and muscle and bone around it—all moved aside in order to accommodate the bullet. The bullet became just another part of my anatomy. It did me no harm.

Then I saw a gallery, a long line of photos in a darkened hall, like the tango hall. Only one of the images—I couldn't see who it was—climbed out of the frame of the photograph and stole away, down the hall, laughing quietly. Then, a moment later, it brought another photo of another girl and hung it where the original had been, tossing away the empty frame.

More dance music, and all the photographs on the wall came to life, stamping, clapping, raising a banging clatter.

I snapped my head up. Someone was hammering on the door with the brass knocker. It had popped me out of my reverie.

I looked around, but Dally was nowhere in evidence, so I assumed she had slipped out while I'd been under. Damn. I finally got a good thing going, and then someone wrecked it.

The racket came again, only more insistent.

I stood up, skipped putting on my shoes as I ordinarily would have. I think it's bad manners to answer a door in your stockinged feet, but the person at the door was obviously in no mood to wait.

I swung the door open just as the noise had reached a fever pitch.

Silent staring for a full ten seconds was followed by a radical mood shift in both faces.

Mine got very genial. His just got madder.

"Detective Huyne. I might have known it would be you."

"What took you so long to get to the door?" He brushed past me and came on into the room.

I closed the door behind him. "I was thinking."

"Uh-huh. Where's Ms. Oglethorpe?"

"I have no idea."

He stared. "Looks like you slept in your clothes again last night."

"Yeah." I looked down at my rumpled condition. "Does look like that, doesn't it?"

"I'm getting a little tired of finding you here when you say there's nothing to your relationship with Ms. Oglethorpe." He was biting his lip, and I could smell the tension.

"I never said there was nothing to my relationship with Ms. Oglethorpe. In fact, quite the opposite. I think there's *everything* to my relationship with her. It's just not the way you mean—or most people mean, for that matter. Maybe you'd find it amusing to know that you and Mickey Nichols share this fascination with the nature of my relationship with the woman in question."

By his expression I gathered that he was in fact not at all amused by this observation. "Well, I'm glad you're here anyway. I have a lot to ask you."

"Look," I began reasonably, "I thought we were going to be friends. You seem very tight just at the moment, and I'd like to see you calm down before we get into what you think you have to ask me."

His face just got harder. "If I kicked your ass right this minute," he whispered harshly, "no one would think a thing about it."

I'll admit to being a little shocked at that observation, but I managed a smile. "I don't know what makes you say that. This is Dally's apartment. She's bound to ask somebody how her living room rug got all messed up. And then there's a certain bartender at Easy who worries about me if I don't show up in good condition after a couple of nights. Not to mention Dane and Mickey, both of whom need me in good shape because they've hired me to help out with a problem they have. So all in all, I think you have underestimated my popularity. But that's not what I'm most worried about. What I really want to know is why you're so bent on doing me harm in the first place. As I have done nothing to you."

He glared like the reflection of noonday sun off hot

chrome. Then, with some effort, his face relaxed. "I'm the competitive sort. That's all. That's what's eating my liver."

"No"—I shook my head—"I'm not playing. What I do is not a competitive sport. It's a wild ride. Still, I think I know what you mean. I know more about the hanging murders than you do. I know more about Janey than you do. And I've been invited to stay in Dally's living room, which you wouldn't mind doing yourself, under the right circumstances. Have I about summed it all up?"

"More or less." But he was not much more amiable than he had been.

"So why don't you sit down, let me put my shoes on, and let's have a nice, slow talk about what the hell is going on? I'm still willing to share information if you are."

Still glaring: "You're a very agreeable sort."

"Yes, I am."

I slipped my shoes on, sat down in the big overstuffed chair, let him take the sofa, and leaned over to tie my laces.

"Did I wake you up," he asked me when he'd settled in, "just now?"

"No. I was really thinking, like I said." No point in explaining the whole trick thing to the guy. He wouldn't get it, that was my guess.

"About?"

"About what do you think? I now have some pretty strange ideas concerning the relationship between Janey and the hanging girls." I wondered then about asking him if he'd ever had any thoughts about the relationship between certain items stolen from the CDC and the murders in question, just to see if he'd tell me or not.

He just nodded, staring me in the eye. "Information you gathered at Beth Dane's apartment—illegally?"

"What makes you think I was in her apartment?" I stared right back.

"Your fingerprints, an eyewitness from downstairs, and Irgo Dane's statement to that fact."

"Yes." I nodded, not looking away. "That does sound convincing. Why Dane would tell you that, I have no idea, but the eyewitness is a break for me, don't you think? I mean, it lets you know that I came into the apartment *after* the murders." I sat back. "I had been a little worried about that, to tell the truth."

"Who's to say you weren't just coming back to remove something—like evidence?"

"Who's to say I wasn't there in my official capacity as an agent of the departed's next of kin? I'm guessing that's pretty much what Dane told you."

"Doesn't matter." He waved his arm dismissively. "You broke and you entered—past police tape. That's not good."

"Still, I was there at the behest of the next of kin, as I was saying, and entered the place in his presence. He was there too." Then, for some reason, I had to push it. "In fact, if your own boys had manifested a little gumption, they might have gotten into the place before me, instead of trying the door once and then lamely deciding it was too hard to get in and putting a little yellow tape across the door. It's just lazy police work."

I could see by his eyes that he was trying to decide whether to stay mad or to laugh.

And because the universe sometimes watches out for guys like me, he busted out laughing.

"You have got to be the most maddening person I've ever run into in any investigation."

"Really?" I was genuinely surprised. "In my line of work I meet tons of people worse than me, or at least *I* think they're worse."

"Well"—he finally sat back, still a little on edge— "as it happens, I just finished chewing out the two officers who put the tape up for more or less the same reasons you've already outlined. It put me behind schedule in my own personal investigation, see?" He crossed his legs. "Now, about this relationship between Beth Dane and Janey you've just mentioned? I think that's all in your head. It's only natural that you'd think that, I suppose, because you're working on the two cases at once, so you might imagine parallels. I don't agree. Except that there was a fair physical resemblance between the two girls, there *is* no relationship."

All I did was shrug. I had no reason to fill him with tales of my strange adventures in the netherworld. He was putting me off, and besides, that was something I needed to spill to Dally.

"But it may interest you to know"—he went on, still a little tightly—"about Mickey. He's a wrong guy, and there's no doubt about that, but I don't believe he killed Janey. You got me to thinking about the MO, and I had to agree with you: Not his speed." He smiled—cold. "So we let him go."

"You let the Pineapple out?"

"We did. Since neither Ms. Oglethorpe nor you would press any other kind of charge, we apologized and drove him home."

"Despite his fingerprints at the scene of a crime?"

He hesitated. Then: "Well, however you would know that information, if you'd think about it, wouldn't you say that his fingerprints would be all over his *girlfriend*'s house no matter what?"

"I guess."

"Anyway, long story short: He's out."

I nodded. "Okay."

"We have a better suspect in jail now anyway." He was trying for a matter-of-fact delivery.

"I don't suppose you'd care to tell me who that might be?"

"Your little rat pal," he said with more meanness than was required, I thought. "Joepye Adder."

21

HEINOUS HANGING HOMICIDES

Now, despite the fact that Joepye had allegedly accused me of the heinous hanging homicides—pardon my alliteration, but it comes from the tabloids. As one might well imagine, the tabloids were having a field day with these particular murders, but I digress. I was still in no mood to have some eager police detective arrest Joe for murders he didn't commit.

"That poor little guy," I told Huyne in no uncertain terms, "can't even organize his own pockets. How's he going to get it together to combine all the talents it would take to pop these kids and then hoist their bodies up a lamppost?"

"He had help."

Oh. "Help?"

"That's right." He eyed me in quite an offensive

manner, and I could tell his blood was rising again. "And I haven't ruled you out, by the way."

"Oh, really? And what possible motive would a person such as myself have for these murders?"

He squinted. "I just said I hadn't ruled you out. That's all. But now that you're reacting this way, it makes me more suspicious, I'd have to say."

"Really. Well." I leaned further forward. "I'd like to officially take back my offer of friendship, if you don't mind." I was talking faster than usual, and I could feel my face flush. "I thought we might share an interest in the grape, a few meaningless hours of discourse on Wallace Stevens, and some repartee vis-à-vis Ms. Oglethorpe. But you've put me right out of the mood. So from now on, you go your way and I'll go mine. Which incidentally means I won't be in the mood to tell you all I know about the tango, so go to Arthur Murray."

I stood for emphasis.

He was staring up at me, momentarily at a loss for words, so I kept right on. "In fact I think I'll be leaving now. And as you are more or less a stranger to me, I'll have to ask you to leave my friend and business partner's home, if you don't mind. Call again someday when you can't stay so long." As they say.

He nodded, stood very slowly, adjusted his coat, folded his arms, and slapped me with a hell-policeman-it's-only-a-matter-of-time stare. "If you withhold *any* sort of evidence in my investigation— even about the tango—I'll see to it that you spend a whole lot of time in the jailhouse. In the second place, you don't have any information worth sharing, I've decided, because it all comes from your little swami act. You don't fool me for a second. You're a second-rate grifter and a third-rate human being, and I have no idea what anybody sees in you. Now out of my way, sonny, before I pop you just for fun."

"Uh-huh." I stood my ground. "Let me explain to you something about the nature of the word *threat*. Since you've been in this house, you've threatened to rough me up once and pop me once—with no provocation on my part. None." I raised my index finger. "So listen carefully: If you so much as accidentally nudge my *jacket* on your way out of this house, I'll be on the phone to IAD before you're off the porch. Have I mentioned my friend and ex-service buddy Detective Winston? He'd believe me if I told him you were no good; he already hates you." I was just guessing, but it stood to reason. Winston hated everybody. "You'd be a private citizen by the end of the month. Then I'd come to your house and kick whatever's left of your skinny ass all over your front yard so the neighbors could get a good look. And I'd do it without much malice. It's just that I think it needs to be done."

Pulling a wild card like Winston was admittedly a hotheaded measure. Winston was notorious. He'd busted more cops out of the force than any other ten Internal Affairs guys put together. He did it because he basically hated cops in general. He was an action junkie, the kind that came back from a lot of hard-core military service. You get your adrenaline and your fear juices up for so long that after a while you can't be comfortable unless you feel that way all the time. Some men join the police force, some become what they call soldiers of fortune, and some become criminals. Winston had managed a little of all three as a top IAD operative. Most people on the Atlanta police force knew who he was, and as luck would have it, he and I were pals.

So, mad as he was, Huyne kept his mouth shut—with some difficulty. I could see him thinking. Then he moved slowly around the sofa to get to the door, avoiding me altogether. But when he got there, he turned around and stared in at me one last time. "You've made a mistake in messing with me."

"Same here, pal." I stared right back.

Big slam.

I looked around the room, my face still flushed. What exactly had I done?

I'd let the guy get to me. Maybe it was because he had interrupted my thing and it had been so hard to get to it that particular time. Or maybe it was some subterranean jealousy that I wasn't willing to admit to myself. It could even have been that we were a little too much alike in some ways, Huyne and I. Those faults we find most distressing in others are often the ones we hate in ourselves.

Mostly I was disappointed in myself because I'd lost my temper. Ordinarily I would have let him rant and just ignored him. What the hell was the matter with me?

Luckily the phone rang before I could sink deeper into the pity festival.

I snatched it up. "Oglethorpe residence."

"So?"

I was very glad to hear her voice.

"Well, Ms. Oglethorpe, how nice of you to call. Where are you?"

"At work, watching them install a new bathroom door. How many bartenders does it take to hang a wooden door?"

"I'm in no mood."

"Three," she told me definitively.

I waited. Then: "Three. Go on. What's the punch?"

"No," she was munching something loudly. "I'm saying three. I'm watching three burly men trying to put up one door—with, so far, scant success."

"You've got to shim a door like that if you want it to balance and hang right."

"Is that so?" She took the receiver away from her mouth. "Have you got it shimmed yet?"

Silence. Then: "What's a shim?"

"Could I just tell you, before the home improvement seminar, that Detective Huyne was just here—and went away mad? And also that Mick is out of the jug, and Joepye is in in his place? And that I might be considered an accessory? And that in the heat of the moment I may have mentioned my old pal Winston to Detective Huyne?" I hesitated. "Oh, yeah, and that I also did my thing and got some good stuff before Huyne interrupted?"

She took a moment to absorb. "You've had a busy morning."

"Yes, I have."

"And you must have been pretty mad—or Huyne must have been leaning pretty hard—to make you bring up Winston."

"Yeah," I said quietly, "I kind of lost it there for a second. He interrupted my thing, see . . . and then he threatened to kick me all over your rug. And I know how you like to keep a tidy appearance—"

"Hold it. He threatened you?"

"I believe his exact words were: 'If I kicked your ass right this minute, no one would think a thing about it.' "

"You explained to him otherwise."

"I did." I smiled into the phone. "I told him you'd care about it, for starters."

"Right," she shot back, "I hate a messy living room."

"That's what I told him."

She took her time. "Well, now I'm mad, and I want to know why he's being such a pistol. And I'm also confused." She shifted the phone. "Joepye?"

"Yeah. How does that make any sense?"

"Well, he did accuse *you*, right?"

"But he probably doesn't even remember that now." I shrugged.

"And finally: You did your thing?"

"Oh"—I picked up a little—"yeah. It was great. I need to talk it out, of course, but I think I may have gotten something."

"Like what?"

"Like why would Joepye be picking my pocket?

And why would Dane be sawing his bass in half? His bass that's shaped very much like a woman?"

"You, my friend"—her voice was amused—"*are* your own little Fellini film, aren't you?"

"Also"—I went right on—"I got shot. Right in the heart. Only I just let the bullet stay there, and it didn't seem to affect me in the slightest."

"Oh." That's all. Just "oh." But I could tell by the sound of her voice I had said something that apparently had a truckload of import, and I didn't have a clue what that might be.

22

THE ALLIANCE

Now, ordinarily when I don't understand something, I just ask. But when it involves Dalliance Oglethorpe and one of her ohs, I generally leave it alone. It'll get back to me when it's ready to be understood.

So I went the safe route. When all about you is chaos and you have no clear vision, the safe route is the one to stay with.

"Well, obviously I need to go over all that with you, right?" I tried to make it sound like just the next sentence in the conversation.

"Right." But her response was, as they sometimes say, perfunctory.

"Can you get away now?" I thought it best to just forge ahead. "I'd really like to keep on the trail while it's hot."

She sighed. "Okay. I guess three burly men can do without my intervention—as long as they figure out what a shim is."

"Words to live by," I told her hastily, "so if you can just make it back to your pad within, say, half an hour, I'll make a few important phone calls and I think I'll have something in the way of an interesting tale to tell."

Her voice warmed again. "I always like that."

"Don't I know it."

"I'll be there in twenty minutes."

"Perfect." And I hung up.

I didn't want to think about the little glimpse of the big picture until I could talk it out loud with Dally, and I *really* didn't want to consider what it was I'd said about it that had momentarily derailed her, so I just went right to the phone work.

There was a time when I kept a lot of numbers in my head. Then, a couple of years ago, I decided that it was getting to be pretty cluttered up there, so I got a notepad instead.

Which is what I pulled out and consulted as I dialed.

I didn't wait long.

"Who is it?" The voice was impatient, but not as mean as it might have been.

"Hello, Mickey, it's Flap Tucker."

"Oh. Flap. Well." He shifted the phone. "How did you know I was out of the can? How did you know I'd be home?"

"I just had something of an uncomfortable visit

from Detective Huyne. Among other things, he told me you were a wrong guy, but then he admitted you didn't pop Janey."

"Imagine my relief."

"I will," I agreed, "but first I'd like to try out a few hunches and run your well-known ways through their paces."

"You want me to find out something."

"In a word, yes." I smiled into the phone, hoping he could hear it. "You're being unusually terse today."

"I have things on my mind." His voice didn't modulate one iota.

"Well, let's try this on for size then. What do you know about Irgo Dane himself?"

"He plays a mean bass. He's kind of stuck up. I hear he's weird."

"That's what I mean." I continued patiently. "Would you happen to know anything about his . . . extracurricular activities?"

"I see." His voice finally demonstrated a little interest. "You want to know what strangeness he's got in him, or perhaps some illicit leanings."

"Exactly."

"That would be an interesting line of inquiry"—he actually lightened up—"considering some of the things I've heard."

"I thought so."

"Because you think he might be connected to the murders of the hanging girls?"

"No. I mean, I don't know." That was honest. "I just had a momentary inkling. I told you, a hunch."

"You did your famous act." He lowered his voice. "You can tell me."

"Well," I said, "I got into it a little ways, and then the aforementioned Detective Huyne interrupted."

"That snake." But it was said without much malice.

"I used to like him better than I do today," I said.

"I will look into this line of thinking and get back with you as soon as I can." He paused. "By the way, I suppose you know that Joepye Adder has taken my place in the can."

"I do know that, yes. Which lowers my estimation of Huyne even further. Like Joepye could manage anything like—"

"Did you know," he interrupted, "that Foggy's troll Daniel Frank was asking around about Foggy's own New Year's Eve party?"

I took a second, then decided that honesty, especially with someone who had recently tried to shoot you, was the best policy. "Yes, he's asking around at my behest. I'm checking on your idea that Beth Dane and Joepye were at the party."

"Good. I thought that might be it." He sounded relieved that I'd told him the truth. I got the impression he'd known the truth all along, and this had been a little pop quiz.

"Why do you ask?" I tried to sound completely innocent.

"Because I just talked to him."

That took a few seconds to digest, considering

what a mighty enmity existed between the two. Then I managed to get out "Daniel?"

"Foggy," he answered. "We have decided to momentarily bury the hatchet, as they used to say out in the Wild West, and try to work together."

Stop the presses. Work together? Mickey "the Pineapple" Nichols and Foggy Moskovitz. "Let me check," I told him, "but isn't that one of the signs of the Apocalypse in Revelation?"

"That is amusing," he told me dryly. "But would you like to crack wise? Or would you instead perhaps care to join us?"

"I'll join." Between Mick and Foggy, just about everything you wanted to know about Atlanta could be known. I was happy to be the third musketeer; it would make my work a snap.

"Good," he answered. "So I propose something of a summit. And since I know without your even saying so that you would wish to have Ms. Oglethorpe involved, why not summitize over at her club? What about sometime around eight o'clock?"

"I'll be there," I assured him.

"Good. I'll alert Foggy." Then his voice got fairly serious again. "I hope Ms. Oglethorpe isn't still sore at me for busting up her bathroom door."

"The door's not all that happy, yet, but Dally seems to be right enough."

"You know, of course, I have every intention of paying for the damage."

"Which you could do," I invited him, "tonight, when we all meet."

"Exactly what I had in mind." There was a commotion on his end. He stayed calm. "So I will be saying good-bye now. Foggy Moskovitz and Daniel Frank have just come in with your friend Paul. They seem to be waving their guns around and insulting everything in sight, so I should probably go now." And he hung up before I could say anything about it.

23

ECLECTICS

I did a lot of pacing and tapping on things for the next few minutes until Dally got home. She hadn't even turned off her car when I came bounding out onto the porch.

"Mickey and Foggy have Paul." I was not calm.

She opened her car door. "What?"

"Daniel's there too. I was talking to Mick on the phone just now, and the last thing he said before he hung up was that they had just come in with Paul and guns."

She stopped still. "That can't be good."

"My thinking exactly."

"Where *was* Mickey?"

"He's home," I told her as I shuffled her back into the car. "And he was driven there by the police themselves, which only makes me suspicious, but I'll deal with that later." One difficulty at a time. We'd solve the question of why the cops had been so friendly *after* we visited the Pineapple at home.

I'd only been to the Nichols mansion once before, but it was quite impressive. He lived in a part of North Atlanta where seven-million-dollar houses were the norm, so his own palace only stood out a little. Greek columns, Italian landscaping, French doors, Chinese carpets, Japanese ponds, and British antiques combined in such a way as to give the impression that a world-traveled diplomat—or an addled art historian—of some sort might live in the house. But I knew for a fact that Mickey hadn't left the southeastern portion of the United States for over ten years.

It must have only taken about a half hour to get to the place, but it seemed like six. Still, I was able to fill Dally in on the highlights of my little internal experience.

When I was finished, she made her usual keen observations. "Well, this time you've really gone off the deep end."

I nodded. "For once, I'd agree to that—even though, as you know, I like the deep end."

"The better to dive into."

"Exactly. But in this case, it actually does seem more like a scene from a cheap Fellini imitation than a clue from the universal unconscious. I mean, look at the picture I'm getting. It's all over the place."

" 'It always is,' " she told me. "Maybe you're tense and trying too hard."

"I think it's the opposite, that I'm not *really* concentrating." I looked out the window. "I think that's the problem."

"You have a lot on your mind."

I blinked. "Hold it."

"What?" She looked around like she'd missed a turn.

"This is more or less the conversation I had with the Pineapple about his shooting pattern in your bathroom door."

"Interesting." She returned her eyes to the road. "You mean you told him the reason he shot up my bathroom door was that he had too much on his mind?"

"No. The reason his *pattern* was so messy was that he had too much on his mind. The reason he shot it in the first place was to keep from shooting *me*."

"Which would have been *lots* messier."

"Right." I turned to look at her. "Lots."

"Still, what's that Zen archery book you made me read?"

"Right. *Zen in the Art of Archery*. Herrigel. A perfect little book. And I see what you mean. Your aim is your aim is your aim."

"To quote Gertrude Stein." She smiled.

"Ah. Erudite patter."

She stole a glance at me. "You're not seriously worried about Paul?"

"Not really," I said, but I sounded anxious even to myself. "But you've got to wonder why Foggy snatched him to begin with. And why there are guns involved."

We were nearing the house.

She pointed. "That's it?"

"Once you've seen it, you really can't forget it."

Most people's houses don't loom the way that house did. It loomed. Even in the clear, cold air, it seemed a little vague and ominous. Maybe because it was just too damned big for a human being to live in.

Most sensible people wouldn't have been quite as bold, but I lumbered right up to the front door and banged.

Seconds later Mickey himself opened the door. "Ah. Tucker. Party of two? You're expected."

I stared. "You were expecting me?"

He stared right back. "What did you think I meant when I said Foggy and Danny had your pal Paul and there was gun waving? I meant for you to come over." Blink. "And you did."

"I see." I peered into the foyer. "And how is that particular situation?"

"Fine."

That was all.

"Fine?"

He smiled. "It seems that our cohorts in this enterprise were concerned about coming into my house unannounced. Given that I have offered to pop Foggy on several occasions, and in fact that I did do some damage to his melon once, I felt I had to be sympathetic about it. Philosophical even."

"I see," I told him slowly. "So the only reason they

were waving guns is that they were just being . . . cautious."

"In a word."

"And Paul's okay?"

He peered in the direction of the study. "Go ask him yourself, why don't you?" He looked past me then. "And Ms. Oglethorpe. What a pleasure it is to welcome you into my humble palace."

"Pleasure to be here," she told him, smiling.

We followed him into the other room. Paul was seated on a thick burgundy art deco–era settee, still in his lab coat work duds, smiling nervously. He seemed relieved to see me.

"Flap."

"Hey, Paul. How's it going?"

"Oh"—he glanced at Daniel, who was standing close to him, still holding his pistol casually at his side—"I can't complain."

I looked around at our company. "Well, this is really something. Who would ever, in his wildest imagination, have thought that this group of people would be standing in this room?"

"Of all the gin joints in all the world." Dally rounded it out.

"So," I continued, "even though I had my mind set on our meeting at Easy a little later tonight, I see that the moment might be ripe for some genuine meeting of the minds."

Foggy still had his pistol out too, but it was resting in his lap. "I'm glad you feel that way." Then he stood slowly. "Ms. Oglethorpe. Please forgive me for not getting up sooner. But this pistol is quite delicate, and I would hate for it to go off accidentally and mess up something in this lovely—if overdecorated—room."

"Overdecorated?" Mickey hung the word in the air.

I took just a moment to reflect that the entire room was in fact a little excessively eclectic.

"You heard me." Foggy turned calmly to face the owner of the room.

Silence.

"I will speak to my interior designer," Mickey answered finally, "when she gets back from Nice. Perhaps we could put our heads together and come up with a more simplified look. I myself have always found it to be a bit"—he glanced amiably around—"much, now that you mention it."

Foggy seemed to relax a little. "Well, Mick, despite our previous encounters, you do genuinely seem to be making the effort in this particular case."

"It's important to me." He looked down at the floor. "Important to both of us, I guess."

Foggy started to speak, then thinned his lips, and finally put away his revolver.

It seemed up to me to act as master of ceremonies. "So. Shall we all have a seat?"

Dally and I sat beside one another in matching Louis XIV–style chairs, not much on comfort, and Mick took a seat with Paul on the sofa. Foggy returned to his secretary's chair by the window box. Daniel kept his place standing beside Paul. It was hard to tell, but I got the impression that Daniel felt he was acting more on Paul's behalf—more like a bodyguard than, say, a kidnapper.

"To business." Mick began. "I believe that everyone in this room has information germane to the matter at hand, to wit: Who iced Janey?"

"And the ancillary: Who hung those two girls up in the park?" Daniel offered matter-of-factly. Then he cast his eye about the company. "Ms. Oglethorpe may have something to offer in that regard, though she might not know it."

"I know *lots* of things that I don't know," she answered him—in a koan I was proud of.

"Precisely." Mick smiled. "So let's get to it."

"First"—Foggy spoke right up, holding up his famous index finger—"let me apologize to everyone for waving this gun about the place." He stole a glance at Paul. "I'm certain if you had seen the side of Mr. Pineapple here to which I have been privy, you would have come in with a little protection too."

"It's okay." Paul's voice was just slightly shaky.

Mickey nodded. "Accepted under the circumstances. But if you don't mind, let me ask the question that is on everyone's mind: Why is this nervous man in a white lab coat here in my house in the first place?"

"Yes." Paul shifted a little to face Foggy. "What about that?"

"He is here in the capacity of the color man," Daniel spoke up, not moving. "I have been asking around, and it comes out that Joepye Adder and Hepzibah—called Beth—Dane were, in fact, uninvited guests at a certain New Year's Eve party a few weeks back. They ate food and drank champagne—"

"Which is fine by me." Foggy picked up. "That's what it was there for. But they also took some snapshots, which is strictly NG in my book. I had too many notables in attendance who would wish to remain anonymous. So I had Daniel here nab the camera—"

"At which point," Daniel finished, "I asked the strange little couple to split. In fact I even had one of our hired security men call them a taxi, because I had been instructed to behave in an extra gentlemanly fashion on that particular evening."

Mick turned to me, nodding approvingly. "It *was* quite a fine affair. Even with all the trouble I caused, everyone treated me discreetly."

"I thought," Foggy pressed ahead, "it might be worth something to see what those two had taken pictures of. So with a little effort, I found the confiscated camera amongst the evening's—shall we say 'lost and found' items?—and developed the film."

Dally leaned forward. I smiled. Foggy was really playing this for the Oscar nomination. He just sat, surveying everyone in the room for a moment, then slowly reached into his coat. A tribute to Mickey's nerve, the Pineapple didn't even flinch.

Foggy produced five shots and laid them out on the table between our chairs and Paul's sofa.

There were three of Janey, one of Mick, and one of a burly man I didn't know.

"Who's the big gent?" I looked up at Foggy.

"Exactly," he said, raising the finger again.

"That," Daniel said, "was one of the outside security men I had hired for the night."

"Yes." Big smile from Foggy. "But his *usual* occupation was security at none other than the Centers for Disease Control here in Atlanta, GA, and his main station was the section where our special guest, Paul, is currently working."

Foggy paused, and it took Paul only a second to realize he was on.

"Oh." He sat up. "Well. The deal is, it looks like the commotion on the outside of the building, my building where I work at the CDC? The night of the theft? That was our boy, Joepye—the commotion. He was drunk and leaning on the buzzer out front and wouldn't go away." He looked at Foggy. "I used to know him, you know. He used to work at Tech with me. He said he was there to say hello to me."

"Ah." Foggy looked at me and raised one eyebrow this time instead of that finger. "The plot, as they say . . ." And he trailed off.

"And the security guard on duty that night," I said, "was this guy, the Charles Atlas guy in the photo."

Paul nodded. "Uh-huh, good guess, and he has since resigned."

"And," Daniel interjected quickly, "disappeared."

"But." That's all Foggy said.

"There's more?" Mick leaned forward, smiling what seemed to be quite the approving smile at Mr. Moskovitz.

Foggy returned the favorable look. "There is." He

sat up straighter. "Tell them what we discussed, Paul."

"Okay, Foggy." Paul's shoulders relaxed, and he exhibited a little wan smile of his own. "Here's the deal: Each one of those toxins that was stolen? In the form that we had it in for travel, it was safe to handle. Get a little on your skin, you wash it off quick and you're okay. But if you happened to inject a *bunch* of it, with a big old needle or something, into a person? That person's esophagus would mostly likely seize up right quick, and that person would suffocate. Toxic shock—you get the same reaction from a lot of things."

"Sort of like, for example," Foggy slipped in quietly, "if they had been choked—if you didn't look too closely."

"Of course," Paul went right on, "the second you did the ordinary toxicology screen on somebody, you'd pick up a good blast of these toxins—"

"If you *did* the test." Mickey interrupted. "But what if the body was cremated or buried before you got to do such a test?"

"Well, then, obviously . . ." Paul started to reply before he realized the rhetorical nature of Mick's question.

"It strikes me"—Mick settled back and lowered his lids in my direction—"that if someone had a gimmick that would help put all these bits and pieces together, *now* would be the time to use same."

"Yeah, Mick." I nodded. "I already tried."

"But Detective Huyne tossed a monkey wrench into your works. You told me on the phone."

"Well"—I stared down at the pictures on the table—"even before that I was shuffling through some pretty strange snapshots of my own. I'm not sure it's working right, my trick."

Mickey put his fingers together. "Why not share? Maybe all of us at once could help with the assembly."

"It's not like that," I told him. "It's not committee work."

"Well, you talk it over with our Ms. Oglethorpe, this odd little experience, don't you?"

"Usually—"

"So why don't you just do that now and let the rest of us . . . overhear?

I looked at Dally. "I feel like I'm in a sideshow."

"Where else would you fit"—she looked around—"in this particular circus?"

Good point. "Okay." I sighed. "In a nutshell: I saw Janey's face, then Beth Dane's face. Her uncle was playing his bass in the background, only with a hacksaw, and the bass was in the shape of a woman's torso—like in that Dali film. While I was watching that, Joepye Adder picked my pocket. Then there was a long line of girls dancing the tango, and spiders crawling on a corpse. Finally there was this gallery, like an art gallery, with a long line of photos, only one of the images, one of the photos, came to life and climbed out of the frame. A second later that person brought another photo of another girl and hung it where the original had been, tossing away an empty frame. Now, the spiders are for the tarantella, obviously, and the tango, from the second note, comes from the scarlet fever toxin because it was from an outbreak in Argentina, where the tango was born. But the rest . . ." I shook my head.

"So," Paul spoke up, "the phrase *nutshell* actually does apply."

Mickey Nichols shook his head. "Okay, my fault. I had no idea what your thingus was like. I get nothing out of it."

The atmosphere in the room had turned strange.

I turned to Dally. "*This* is why I don't like to discuss it."

"So why did you?" she asked me, reasonably.

"Everyone insisted." I shrugged. "Plus, I thought it might help. It seems to be bummed up somehow, my so-called thingus. I thought maybe if I exposed it to a little more scrutiny . . ."

"The third poison." Foggy had stood up.

We all looked at him.

"You saw spiders and tangos—that's the first two toxins. The third one's still out there."

It seemed to take us all a little too long to follow his thinking.

Dally was, as usual, the first to get there. "There's going to be another murder."

24

LOBSTER LEASH

Only a few minutes later, still against everyone's loud better judgment, Dally called Detective Huyne. It didn't take long for him to come to the phone—once he knew who was calling.

"Sorry to bother you," she started quickly, "but you know about the three stolen toxins from the CDC. Flap's come up with a plausible connection between two of them and the two hanging murders, so it occurred to us that—"

He'd obviously interrupted her, and she shot me a look.

Then: "That's right." She nodded. "I see. Well . . . there you are then."

She smiled at something else he was saying.

Finally she nodded. "Okay, see you then." And she hung up.

"So?" I stared.

"So he was way ahead of us. He's having the perimeter of the park staked out so he can nab the people before they hang the third victim." She blinked. "How's that for . . . something?"

"Good for the police," Foggy began, "but of course—"

"That will be just about one step too late for the actual victim." I finished.

"They're already dead," Foggy tried explaining to Mickey, "before they get hoisted."

"I *know* that." Mickey sounded a little irritated. "You think I'm thick."

Dally smiled. "Before that line of conversation gets way out of control, may I suggest that Mr. Tucker has some further work to do?"

We all looked at her.

"She's right," Mick said. "You've got to figure out who will get iced next—before the actual event."

Foggy nodded. "You've got to prevent another murder."

Daniel gave his mute assent.

I tried not to succumb to the urgency of the situation. That's just the sort of thing that makes my little trick fly away like a scared night bird. But I could see, just on the periphery of my unconscious, another dancer swinging in the cold January air.

"Do you have, maybe," Dally suggested to Mick,

"a quiet room where Mr. Tucker can get away from it all?"

"Indoors or out?" He directed the question at Dally, like she was my agent.

"Flap?" She went straight to me.

"Anyplace is fine. It's a little cold to go outside," I said, "but look, I'm not sure it'll work. It's been kind of on the blink."

"Do your best. That's all you can do." Foggy was very philosophical, I thought, with my unconscious.

"This way." Mick indicated, and I followed.

I followed him down a darker hallway to a small study that seemed set for a play; nothing in the room looked like it had ever been used for any real function. It was a set piece.

Mick turned to me. "I always thought this room would be nice for a quiet moment—if I ever got around to one."

I nodded. He split.

So. Stranger in a strange land, I sat on a nice thirties-style overstuffed chair facing out the window: bare black tree limbs, overcast sky—perfect.

I breathed in through my nose, imagining the air curling upward through my skull and then subsiding, like a wave, into the pit of my stomach. In. Out. In. Out. The bare limbs seemed to sway in the same rhythm. The curtains on either side of the window seemed to flutter, though the window was closed. Gold began to steal into the corners of my eyes, and even when I blinked once or twice, it was still there.

Suddenly there was a rush of images like one of those art film collages: barely discernible pattern; difficult-to-catch innuendo. Then it all slammed shut, and I was in the park with Joepye Adder at my side. He was holding a dog leash attached to a lobster that was trying to crawl away from him on the sidewalk.

The corpse was swaying in an angular fashion. She was moving in a little box step, hanging from the lamppost in the icy morning air. I was staring up at it.

"What exactly is that thing tied around her neck?"

"That's an apron, Flap."

Snap.

I was right out of the the scene and back into Mickey's unused study. I stood and beat it to the door.

"Dally?"

They all heard the sound of my voice, and the urgency in it, and they all appeared in the hall.

"What?" She got to me first, hand on my shoulder.

"Is Joepye still in the lockup, did Huyne say?"

"He didn't say."

"Joepye?" Foggy's face betrayed a mild disbelief.

I tried to take them all in, standing in the darkened hall. "Joepye had something more to do with all this than I thought." I shot a look at Dally. "And our friend Minnie is somehow involved too."

Paul's voice was quiet. "You got all that in two minutes?"

"Let me sit down, and I'll explain it, if I can."

We all adjourned back into the parlor, took our seats, and I caught a few deep breaths.

"Remember," I began, facing Dally, "my little bit of esoterica about the French writer Gérard de Nerval?"

"The guy who hanged himself by an apron string, right." She nodded.

Everyone else just looked confused.

"Do you remember the first time," I asked her, "that I brought it up?"

"Should I?"

"When Minnie was over at your place one night last year—don't remember when—and she was telling us about this idea for her show, the photo exhibition built around the Billie Holiday tunes."

"Really?" She sounded skeptical.

I nodded. "You told her she should include 'Strange Fruit,' one of the few songs Billie actually wrote herself, and I brought up the ancillary image of Nerval hanging from a lamppost."

"Last summer." She nodded slowly. "After the party at her place."

"I guess." I shrugged.

"Man"—she looked at me—"I would never have remembered that."

"That's the benefit of my little gag," I explained, tapping my forehead. "It's all up there, you just have to get at it."

"How is this about Joepye?" Mick seemed impatient. "I thought we believed he had nothing much to do with all this."

I squinted. "Joe's been drinking for a good while

now, and he can barely see straight anymore. And he was loaded the night he took me to find the first dancer. But *he*'s the one who saw that she was hanging by an apron string."

"And your eyesight, in fact your perception in general, is far superior to his, you're saying." Foggy nodded.

"At least," I confirmed.

"Joepye already *knew* it was an apron." Dally's voice was very cold.

"That's what I'm thinking," I told her, "and I've got to believe he somehow knew about the Nerval deal. Maybe I told it to him or maybe—here's a far-fetched notion—Minnie told him about it."

"Who is this Minnie?" Paul wanted to know.

I turned to him. "She's a kid from the Atlanta College of Art, over at the High Museum—"

"And the second victim." Dally finished, still very chilly-sounding.

"Well, I'll be." Daniel nodded.

"What?" I said.

"Well, in my poking around about Joepye and Beth Dane being at my party? It could be just a coincidence, but Beth Dane? One of her odd jobs when she wasn't . . . *entertaining*? She was a life model at the Atlanta College of Art."

Foggy leaned in Mickey's direction. "She would pose in the nude for the students."

Mickey turned to me. "Do you see why I might want to bust this guy in the head? He's always treating me like I don't know shinola." Then he looked at Foggy. "I know what a life model is, Ignatz."

"Ignatz?" Foggy was amused. "Is that that supposed to be some sort of insult?"

"Take it how you like." Mick's voice was harsher.

"Boys." Dally jumped in. "Put a collar on all that for two seconds, could you?" She whipped her head around to face me. "I already know what you think of coincidence. Didn't you mention some charcoal sketches at Beth's hovel?"

I was right with her. "There's a connection between Minnie and Beth . . . and Joepye. Even if it's just that they met when Minnie was sketching Beth in life class at college, right?"

"I'll admit," Mickey said slowly, "that I don't quite get all this. Are you saying that Joepye *is* the murderer?"

"Not likely." I started slowly. "I still think he doesn't have the wherewithal to manage this kind of a scene, let alone think it up in the first place. Still, he had *something* to do with all this."

Dally squinted. "But he had help, you're implying."

"Yes." I said it like I knew what I was talking about. "Somebody who could think it all up, manage to move around a lot of the paperwork involved at the police station, for example, hustle things through the system—an operator."

"Who?" Mick looked suspiciously at Foggy.

Foggy returned the look in spades.

But Dally's eyes gradually got bigger. "You're not

suggesting . . ." She turned her head my way like the slow and certain advent of dawn. "It couldn't be."

"Yes, it could." I stood and moved for the door. It suddenly all made sense: why he'd be so hot with me for no apparent reason. "It could very well be that not-so-secret-admirer of yours, Burnish Huyne."

25

AN ACTOR PREPARES

Ordinarily I like to think of myself as a live-and-let-live sort of person. But when someone's living interferes with someone else's being alive, I occasionally get involved.

And in this particular case, I felt I had to speak directly with the man in question. Dally did all manner of insisting, but in the end I dropped her off at the club and went home to call Huyne on my own. Better to aim your arrows without anyone looking over your shoulder.

So:

"Huyne." He sounded tense.

"Detective." I tried to sound jolly. "It's Flap Tucker."

"What is it? Ms. Oglethorpe already called and

told me your news flash, like everybody in town didn't already know there could be a third murder in the offing."

Ah, so he was still not in the best of moods. "Well," I began soothingly, "maybe I have something else to offer."

He obviously wasn't buying. "Like you said, I can look it up. Now, if there's nothing else—"

"As a matter of fact, there is." *What the hell*, I thought, *dive in*. I've often gotten *brave* and *stupid* confused. Since I was on the phone where he couldn't get at me right away. I was wrong he'd maybe laugh. I was right he'd probably come after me. Even better. Then I could maybe trick him up and finish our tale as the hero. So I dove: "I have the crazy idea in my mind that you yourself have something to do with these murders."

Silence. He didn't immediately object. So I dug a deeper hole. "I don't say this out of any malice. I just think that hustling paperwork through the police bureaucracy seems to have played a key part in all these proceedings—what with the laughable assertion that these kids are suicides, for example, and you're at the heart of that possibility."

Still no response, which only meant trouble, I thought. But I kept hammering. "Not to mention, on a personal level, your strange change of heart in our relationship as I got closer and closer to the actual foundation of the events."

Long moment of silence.

"Finished?" He didn't even sound perturbed.

"Well . . ." because I wasn't finished.

"Before you go on, I want you to know that I think this is the first honest conversation we've had since the other night over at Easy. Now, as long as we're sharing, I think that your main beef with me has something to do with Dalliance Oglethorpe and not a genuine suspicion of murder."

He was wrong, but I let him go on.

"Now, I also think it's interesting that you and I have come up with some relatively similar theories about what's going on, and we've each suspected the other of being more involved than either of us probably is."

"Diction aside"—I smiled coldly into the phone—"I'm with you."

"So let me assure you that if I were on the outside looking in, I'd suspect me too, or *somebody* here in the office. Not of the murders, maybe, but of complicity, most assuredly."

"Okay." I thought I sounded like I believed what he was saying. "So are we back to being pals?"

"We were never *pals*," he said, "but I think we can probably drop all the crap and try working together again—to get all this swept up. It's a big mess now."

"Now?" I had to laugh. "It wasn't a mess before?"

"It's a whole lot more confusing now than it was when this was just another hooker suicide." I heard the strangeness in his voice.

"Yes. Well." I took a deep breath. "You certainly are full of surprises, I'll give you that." Turning up the disingenuity: "Why, I half expected you to explode

through the phone and come after me with a big police gun."

"Could still happen," he said easily. "But for now I
think we have to go to work, don't you? Save the fun
for later. Can you meet me around five-thirty?"

"Where?"

"You know the overpass bridge by the small lake
at the park?"

It was a place generally littered with boys' under-
wear and used condoms. "Only in passing. You want
to meet *there*?"

"It's one of our stakeout points."

"Oh. Okay." I tried to sound convinced. "See you
there at five-thirty."

We hung up.

I had never been so completely convinced of my
mistrust of another person in my entire adult life. That
bridge was too obviously the perfect place to rub out a
person such as myself who had stuck his nose in where
it didn't belong. And I called up Dalliance Oglethorpe,
as I'd promised to do, and told her just that.

"And he wants you to meet him *where*? Under that
lovers' bridge?"

"Right," I nodded, "just a little over an hour."

"You're not thinking of going. It's obvious—"

"Of course I'm going." I was firm in that resolve.
"How else am I going to get the goods on the guy?
Action, that's what we want now."

"Not by yourself, you're not going, Mr. Action."

"Yeah, well." I shifted the phone to my other ear.

"I was thinking I'd give Daniel a call. He's handy in a situation like that."

"Oh, *that*'s a good idea." Her voice was dripping with what literary types still refer to as irony. "Take a hood to a dark bridge at sunset and gun down a cop. Get arrested and go to prison. See do I care. I won't wait for you if you get more than twenty years. I've told you that before."

"You certainly are jumping to a boatload of conclusions." I was calm. "I just want Daniel to hang around on the periphery . . . in case. And all I have in mind is confronting the detective with his own evil ways. I'll also tell him you know all about it, and that'll give him pause, see? Plus, I'll use that tape recorder you gave me awhile back to memorialize our little confab."

"You've still got that little pocket recorder I got you for your birthday?"

"Sure," I told her. "Why do you sound so surprised? I love your gifts."

"But you never use them. When's the last time you used those expensive antique file cabinets?"

"It's holding up a fine small wine rack even as we speak."

"For your files, Flap. When's the last time you used them for your *files*?"

"Oh. Well, truth be told, that hasn't taken hold yet—"

"Never mind. I'm glad you're using the tape recorder."

"It's neat."

"I could leave Hal in charge of the club this evening," she slipped in. "We're not that crowded."

"You know how much you worry about me in situations like this? Well, I worry about you twice as much. Mostly because I'm a bigger worrier. You're a much more stable person. Besides, I'll need someone to phone in case I get shot up. And if you're all shot up too, who do I call?"

"This is making me feel better." More of that irony.

"You know what I'm saying?"

"I do," she said, "and I don't like it."

"Okay, don't like it then. I'll call you the second it's all over." I could hear the background noise in the club. "Besides, it sounds like you've got work to do."

"That's just the boys finally getting the new men's room door to close all the way." She sipped something. "We're celebrating."

"Okay, have one for me, and I'll call you in a few hours." I almost hung up. "Dally?"

"What?" She was trying to sound like she was calm.

"This isn't that big a deal. Huyne might be evil, but he doesn't seem to be stupid, does he? He's not going to pop me in the park—not when *you* know all about it, and that's going to be the first thing out of my mouth when I see the guy. So."

"Okay." She did sound a little better.

Which only proves that maybe I should have stayed in the theatre-life. I was just that good an actor.

26

BLACKBIRD BRIDGE

At five twenty-five the sun was just beginning to go down behind the bare tree limbs. I'd parked over by the bathhouse and walked deliberately toward the lake and the bridge. I hadn't seen any evidence of a stakeout, but then, if the guys had been doing their jobs, I guess I wouldn't. So I tried to pretend that everything was jake.

Daniel Frank had been out when I'd called him, so I was solo. I didn't feel I had time to waste looking for him.

The park was nearly empty. The lake was a dull, thick gray; matched the sky almost exactly. The black branches spilled out over the sky and the surface of the water like spilled ink. The air was cold, but a little too humid to be crisp. Humidity in January: there's the South.

Since I'd been off-kilter for a few days at that point, the extreme adrenaline rush I felt was just one more strange biochemical convolution in a long list of things that were messing me up.

Still, it made me especially alert. Before I'd even reached the edge of the lake, I heard some rustling in the leaves that sounded like somebody walking around. All I could see were shadows, but the shadows were alive, and when I walked a little farther, the noise stopped suddenly, and the air was still. The only sound, besides the pounding in my temples, was the scrape of my soles on the sidewalk that ran to the bridge.

I stopped about three yards shy of the actual overpass and just stared. Down the ravine to my left was a thicker woods, an occasional hobo jungle; sometimes a lovers' lane. Seemed deserted, but in the shadows, who could tell for certain? To my right, the still waters of the little lake lay sullen and gray.

Stillness. Breathe in, breathe out. Let him make the first move. Let him come to me.

When you relax like that, around a center of almost explosive tension, it can be very expanding. I felt my peripheral vision, for example, registered just at a full 360 degrees, and I could have sworn I heard the beating of little cricket hearts in the black shadows.

I don't know how much time passed like that—could have been thirty seconds, could have been half an hour—but finally Burnish Huyne made his play.

"Okay, obviously you know I'm here." His voice was edgy.

I didn't move, but I placed his voice just under the first left column of the overpass.

"You make a great target, standing there with the light behind you."

Still, all I did was breathe. What did I care? Bullets bounced off me . . . when I was in that particular frame of mind.

"That *is* you, right, Tucker?" More nervous. Good. And the sun behind me obviously obscured my face. Better.

Finally he came out of the shadows. He had a gun in his hand, but it was pointed at the ground. It was a small snub nose—obviously not his police weapon.

"Flap?"

"Hello, Burnish." First names, I noted. "Dally says hey."

Big sigh from his direction. "Okay, it *is* you."

"That's a surprise?" I still didn't move. Didn't want to make him any more nervous than he was. "You asked me to meet you here, remember?"

"Yeah . . ." He trailed off.

"So?"

"Come over here."

I shook my head. "Not really. Why don't you come out in the light?"

"Because I've got something to show you."

I smiled. "That's the wrong thing to say, especially to a convicted heterosexual such as myself, at this *particular* bridge."

"Yeah." He laughed a little. "I guess you're right. Still. I have to ask you to come over here."

"Put your little toy gun up first."

He looked down. "Oh." Back at me. "I forgot I had it in my hand."

"Uh-huh."

He shoved it back in his shoulder holster and held out both hands so I could see they were empty. "Okay?"

I held my ground. "What did you want to show me?"

"Believe it or not, it's paperwork."

I looked around. Over by the bathhouse I'd seen a blur, and when I looked, I could see two guys in jogging suits trying very hard to look natural. So there actually was a stakeout in progress. Better and better.

I tilted my head in their direction. "Friends of yours?"

He smiled. "I'd say about one in fifty undercover types really knows what he's doing. The rest, you can always make."

"Right."

"They're keeping an eye on that part of the street by the gazebo."

I nodded. "I can see that."

He lowered his voice. "That's why I want you to come over here. I don't need anybody knowing my business."

"So why meet here in the first place?"

"I'm not like you." His voice was tough and relaxed for the first time; he was getting back to his old self. "I occasionally have to go where I'm told. I've got a boss."

"I see."

"I'm supposed to be the head of this investigation, on the periphery of which you seem to be lurking."

"Right," I told him. "But I feel I'm more in the actual center of things. Of course, philosophically speaking, everybody feels more or less in the center of things. I mean, from your own perspective, you *are* the center of the universe, after all."

"I am?" He shook his head. "Doesn't feel that way very often."

And that's the sentence that made me walk toward him. I figured a person who was willing to examine himself at least to that extent deserved to be considered a genuine human being—somebody, in short, who might not plug me the first chance he got.

"So *what* paperwork?"

He seemed relieved that I was joining him in his little hideaway. "Two files, really, are all I brought with me. But I think they reflect the bigger picture."

Under the bridge he had a thermos, a short folding stool—further evidence of the stakeout—and a briefcase. He'd opened the case and pulled out two manila folders before I'd reached his spot.

"I got all this stuff together when you mentioned your friend Winston. It occurred to me to start thinking like IAD. This is Beth Dane's short file." He didn't even look up at me. "These are are her prints, the ones we used to identify the body. They were on file already from a couple of vice busts, right?"

"I see." I came under the bridge. The final auburn light from the west spilled over the police sheets.

"Now, the thing is—and I know this is probably my imagination—but take a look at the prints."

I did. "All fingerprints look pretty much alike to me. I don't have your discriminating eye. Enlighten me."

"Look at the thumb here, for example." He pointed.

"So?"

"Doesn't it seem kind of . . . small?"

I peered closely at it. "I guess."

"Almost like a kid's print, instead of an adult's."

"Beth Dane wasn't much of an adult, was she?"

"Twenty-three," he said.

"So . . ."

"So, still, Beth Dane was a big girl, wasn't she?"

"I never met her." Except after she was already dead.

"Dane's a big man, though."

I nodded. "That's right. Probably six five and at least two hundred fifty pounds."

"She'd have to have freakishly small hands"—he looked back down at the page—"to make prints that small." He looked up at me. "Did you notice that her hands were abnormally small?"

"Under the circumstances," I said, "the fact that she was swinging from a lamppost and her face was black and bloated really occupied as much of my mind as I could give to the event."

"No," he told me firmly, "that's not you. You take

in these little details, whether you register them consciously or not. I've heard the stories." He stared at my hat. "You've got a computer up there."

"It's never been put quite that way." I smiled. "Probably because it's not true. But I know what you're getting at." He wanted a peek at my trick too. "I'm sorry to report that nothing along the lines of what you're talking about has come to me. I got no images of tiny hands."

Big shrug. "Well, here's the other thing. More in the line of confirmation." He pulled out another file. "Minnie Moran? She died of toxic shock, overdose of scarlet fever Dick test vaccine."

"The outbreak in Argentina. The tango."

"Right. So this stakeout really means something. The third toxin—the rabies thing—is still out there. I guess that's pretty much along the lines you've already figured out."

"Hate to bring this up"—I looked at the ground—"because I know how you like to jump to conclusions where Mickey Nichols is concerned, but I have to tell you that he sent me a little note about that very vaccine just yesterday and seemed to know the murders and the toxins were connected."

"Oh, really?" He stared at my profile.

"Yes, but in all fairness, he might have gotten the idea from your journal."

"My journal?"

"That's right. Here's how it worked." I looked up at him. "Mickey's got guys all over. Even all over your station house, it would seem. One of them sees you're working on your journal, gets a shill who says hello to you in some distracting way, while the other guy walks behind you, swipes a gander at whatever it is you're writing, and it's all over in two seconds. You go back to writing without ever even knowing." I blinked. "He compared it to picking pockets."

"Jesus."

"So he's very suspicious of you—and how you knew there was a connection between the toxins and the murders. And he's infected me with the same paranoia."

"You don't trust me?"

"Not one bit." I met his eyes.

He stared hard. "Then it was kind of stupid of you to come out with me today."

"But I had to know." I smiled. "I had to know about you."

"And *do* you now?"

"Not really." It was getting harder to see him in the shadows, and the light was fading fast.

"What can I do to assure you?" His voice was anything *but* reassuring.

"Well." I blew out my breath, and it made a little ghost. "How about a little Wallace Stevens."

I'd clearly surprised him.

"You told me the other day that you were a Wallace Stevens fan. Was that just to impress Ms. Oglethorpe, or do you really know anything about the greatest American poet of the twentieth century?" I'd said it mostly to throw him off-balance. That, at least, had worked. But I also really wanted to see if he actually knew any of the poetry. I was betting that he didn't.

He stared. Then he put the files back in his brief-case and set the case on the ground between his ther-mos and his seat.

" 'I was of three minds,' " he began, " 'Like a tree In which there are three blackbirds.' Know it?"

" 'Thirteen Ways of Looking at a Blackbird'? Sure. One of my faves, if something of a *pop* choice, from the body of the artist's work. Why that line?"

"Seemed right," he said, suddenly reaching for his inside coat pocket, "since I still can't decide whether to trust you, arrest you, or shoot you dead."

27

SMOKE ON THE WATER

The last of the light was nearly gone. I couldn't see Huyne's face, but I could see his gun just fine.

"A guy like me," I began in a very matter-of-fact manner under the circumstances, "believe it or not, can go sometimes a whole year without even seeing a gun. And here this is my second look at one in the same week. What do you make of that?"

He stared. "Maybe you're just associating with the wrong crowd."

"That could be it." I stuck out my lower lip. "But I think it's more because of the general angst of January."

He lowered the gun a little, and I got the impression he thought he hadn't heard me correctly.

"January," I went on, "contrary to poetical opinion, is the cruelest month. It's supposed to be a brand-new year, but in general most people experience the same old things. And they're suffering from holiday hangover—I mean, the psychological kind—so they're extra vulnerable to an attack of angst. See?"

"Not even remotely, so shut up." He stepped out from under the bridge. "Let me get right to the point. You didn't react to my little news here the way I thought you would."

"So," I smiled, "this *was* something of a test."

"It was."

"And I didn't pass?"

"You didn't register."

"Why?" That stumped me.

"I thought you were either going to be tremendously surprised and curious about the fingerprint evidence, or you were going to start in with all manner of explanation. The former would have told me you were clean, the latter that you were hiding something."

"I see," I told him. "So I didn't play the game the way you wanted me to."

"Right."

"And now you don't know what to make of me."

"Right."

"Well"—I shifted my weight to one leg—"that makes two of us."

The gun went lower still. "Sorry?"

"I say, I don't know what to make of you either, and this little scene has only made me more uncomfortable about you."

"What are you talking about? You still think I'm in with the killer?"

"I still think that maybe you're more involved in this whole mess than you ought to be," I said. "Although maybe I'm waxing naive here, in light of the fact that you're the one with the gun. Still, there are cops all around apparently, and you're certainly smart enough to realize that Ms. Oglethorpe knows exactly where I am . . . and is looking to hear from me within the hour."

He paused long enough for my adrenaline to get stirred up a little more and for my eyes to dart left for a second, as I thought about where I'd dodge just in case he started to fire his little pistol. No need in testing my bullet-bouncing theory in the middle of the January Angst Festival, after all.

Slowly, almost outside the realm of possible human movement, I saw the gun coming back up, and a little closer, headed toward pointing itself at my heart. I took a slow, silent breath in through my nostrils and concentrated hard on his eyes. Most people who've shot a gun more than once usually tense their eyes just before they squeeze the trigger—something about muscle memory from the previous noise and thrust of the firing gun.

The air seemed to grow more humid, and then the light was gone. We were silhouettes under a stone bridge in the first shadows of the night. It occurred to me that it wouldn't be the worst time to consider taking up old-fashioned prayer.

"Hey!"

A voice shot out across the lake so suddenly I thought for a split instant that Huyne had fired his gun. He flinched too.

"Detective Huyne! Quick!"

He lowered the pistol.

I called out, "What is it?"

He shot me a look, then moved around me to the sidewalk just above us. "Who's calling?"

"It's Conway. Over here, by the ball field!"

He moved more quickly than I would have thought possible. I followed.

We ran across the street that separated the bathhouse from the big stone steps. The steps ran up to the baseball and soccer fields. The lampposts blinked on all at once, and suddenly a cold, eerie light washed over everything. I was only three or four steps behind Huyne. He still had his gun in his hand.

We took the steps three at a time, and once we were halfway up, we could see the fields—and the cause of all the commotion. There was a third body hanging from the post on the other side of the fields, close to Piedmont Road.

We ran faster. We both slowed only a little just before we got there, but I was pretty winded. Four or five cops were already there, staring up at the victim.

Before he was even among them, Huyne started yelling, "How the *hell* could this happen with everybody and his brother watching? Who was here at the road?"

A beefy young guy raised his hand. "I was over by the Driving Club, about half a block away, sir." He sounded scared. "I seen the car pull up, and I headed this way, you know, because it ain't no parking on the street here. And then I seen somebody get out with a big bundle, and then they came in here where I couldn't see for the trees and all, and three seconds later, I swear, they was back out and drove away real fast down Piedmont going north."

"Just one person?"

"Yes, sir." The kid was still breathing hard from the run. Everybody was.

I was surprised to see Huyne turn my way. "How could one person carry a body, hoist it up like this, and get back out in that kind of time?"

I stared up at the body. Even though it was hard to see because you had to look right into the lamp, you could tell there was something wrong with it. The way it moved, the way it hung.

"Detective?" I was squinting into the light.

"Yes?" He was not sounding patient.

"That's not a body."

Everybody looked.

"What?" Huyne's voice was as irritated as I'd ever heard it.

"It's nothing like the other two." I was watching how easily the little bit of breeze was moving this one. "I think it's a dummy."

Guys started moving around underneath it and shading their eyes to get a better look.

One of the feet fell off.

The shoe, stuffed with an empty sock, came plummeting to the dirt.

Then one of the men, before someone could tell him not to, jumped up like a basketball player and swatted at the thing.

The pants, filled with wadded-up newspaper, swung away and came to land a few feet south of our little group.

"Cut it out!" Huyne shouted. "Conway, go get the damned ladder!"

Conway hustled away.

Huyne shook his head. "What the hell?"

I was still staring up at the torso. "It's got a note, though—like the others."

"Why would somebody do this?"

"It's a copycat." One of the officers ventured the suggestion.

The beefy guy shrugged. "Just kids, having fun."

"Quiet, all of you." But Huyne's voice was more calm. "Let's let Mr. Tucker give us his opinion."

"Me?" I shrugged. "What makes you think I've got an opinion?" I looked up. "But I would like to read that note."

We all fell silent. A couple of awkward minutes later Conway returned with an aluminum stepladder.

Huyne himself stepped up it, while three others held. The detective glanced at the note, made a crude remark, and then reached up to unhook the rest of the dummy from the lamppost.

He dropped it and got down the ladder fast.

The torso fell face up—if you could call panty hose crammed full of balls of newspaper a face—and the note presented itself for us all to see.

" 'Dance, Scarecrow.' " The beefy guy was apparently the kind of person who read better out loud. He looked up. "Huh?" Then at me, for some reason. "What's it mean?"

Huyne jumped the last step and stood over the top half of the scarecrow. Very softly: "What the hell?"

I smiled. "Well, I think that's enough for me." I looked over at Huyne. "Unless you have any more tests for me, I'd like to head on home now."

"You want to go home *now*?" He jutted his chin in my direction. "With all this?"

"All what?" I looked around. "This is just somebody, maybe not even the murderer, playing the police for saps—if you'll excuse my saying so. As I am not a policeman, I think this is more your party than mine. Besides, I promised I'd call Dally, remember?"

He gave out with a big sigh, and it trailed white in the cold air, but he finally nodded. "Okay." Then he took a quick step toward me. "But no talking with her about our earlier discussion, right? It's police business. And I'll be checking in with you later tonight."

"I'll be at the club," I told him. "And I'll tell Dally everything. I always do."

He stared at me for a second longer, then decided it wasn't worth his time to keep messing with me, so he made a face and waved his hand. "Get lost."

"Can do." I nodded, turned back toward the bathhouse, and strolled away in the evening air.

Stars were beginning to blink on, and there was a nice moon, still nearly full. I had shuffled down the stone stairs and headed for where my car was parked before I saw the fire.

It was just a small orange blaze a little left of the bridge. The smoke was drifting south, out over the little lake. I stopped in my tracks. The fire was burning exactly where I'd been standing with Detective Huyne only moments earlier, and I was pretty certain that I knew *what* was burning.

Even though all I really wanted to do was just head for the car, not stop until I hit my stool at Easy, and have a glass of something red, still, I turned around and hiked right back up the steps again.

At the top I waved my arms and shouted, "Hey! Huyne! Fire!"

I don't think they heard me at first. Even though the night air carries sound pretty well, you just don't expect a man to be yelling "fire" on a cold, damp night.

But they headed my way. I was obviously shouting something and waving my arms, and Huyne came toward me at a pretty good clip. I decided to wait for him. He was just the sort of person who might get the mistaken impression that I could be the guy who *started* the fire, and I didn't need that.

He got close before I turned in the direction of the bridge. "Fire. By the bridge."

He picked up his pace, got to my side, stared, then registered. "Oh, my God. My files."

We all ran toward the orange glow. I had a second of thinking how comical we all must have looked to someone far off, a little like the old Keystone Kops, running back and forth like idiots.

The flames were already dying out by the time we got to the bridge. Huyne's briefcase and his folding stool were charred black, and the thermos had exploded. There were pieces of it all around.

Huyne kicked at the mess, and it was clear that the files were completely destroyed.

He looked up at me. "I guess you didn't see who started this?"

I shook my head. "It was cooking by the time I got to the stairs back there."

"Damn." He stared down at the smoking mess.

"Those were just copies, right?" I stared with him.

"Sure, but—"

"But what?" I asked when he wouldn't finish his sentence.

"There were things in there that I *can't* replace. My notes, some phone numbers." He looked around at the cops. "You all fan out from here, see if you can get anything. Footprints, pack of matches—anything."

The policemen moved immediately to search the area, and Huyne stepped close to me.

"Somebody's been messing with these files already, see?" he said, barely above a whisper. "Little things out of place. No one but me would notice. And this scene, the dummy, the fire." He stared into my eyes. "What the hell's going on, Flap?"

"I hate this," I began. "I mean, I hate telling you what I'm about to tell you, but you know what made the Scarecrow dance?"

"What?"

"Fire." I shrugged. "The witch throws the fire at the Scarecrow, and he dances."

"What the hell are you talking about?"

"*Wizard of Oz*. I don't care for it personally, but Dally watches it every time it's on television. Every time. One of her rare girl things, that's how I explain it to myself."

"*Wizard of Oz?*"

"The Scarecrow is afraid of fire."

He took a beat, and he was still edgy. "This explains the dummy and the fire?"

"Maybe."

"I don't buy that." He shook his head. "It's like something a kid would do. A weird little kid."

"Yeah," I told him, "or an adult somebody whose mind was like that always."

He snapped his head up again and shot me a look. "Adder."

I nodded again. "Well, that's what I'm thinking. But you've got him in lockup, right?"

He craned his head around until he caught the eye of the nearest cop and beckoned. "Come over here for a second, would you?"

The cop came over, and Huyne continued. "Check in with Verna downtown, please, and make sure Joe Adder is still in lockup, okay?"

The guy cranked up his shoulder radio, talked a little, made small talk, and waited.

I looked at the ashes. "Why'd they put the thermos in? They had to know it'd blow up."

"Maybe they *wanted* it to," Huyne said, staring down at the pieces. "Maybe they knew it would blow up and somebody would catch the shrapnel."

"Well, *that* doesn't sound like Joepye."

"And poisoning young girls so he can hang them up in the park? That does?"

"Okay." I nodded.

The cop who'd called into the station house turned around. "He made bail, Detective."

We both jerked our heads in his direction.

"Bail?" Huyne sounded sick. "When? No, wait. Ask them who?"

He smiled. "Already did. Thought you'd want to know. It was somebody named Dames."

"Dane?"

"Could have been." The cop nodded.

"I think that's what she said, something like that. And it was around three hours ago, maybe more."

"Jesus, he's out." Huyne turned my way. "It's Adder." Still sounded a little sick. "He's the one."

"I don't really *want* to agree with you," I told him. "But I do." Then I turned and started toward my car.

"Wait. Where you going now?"

"Same as before: Dally," I called out over my shoulder. "I've really got to talk to her. Come on over to the club when you're done here, why don't you? We've still got plenty to talk about too, don't we?"

"Yeah, I guess we do." He turned back to the smoking briefcase. "I'll be over after a while." Then suddenly: "Hey. Why did *Dane* bail him out?"

"Right." I said. "That's just one of the things I'd like to know."

All I could think about was the image in my little dream state of Dane sawing a naked woman in half like he was playing his bass. I had just realized that the tune he'd been playing was in fact "Over the Rainbow."

28

STRAYS

I couldn't decide which I needed most: another crack at doing my trick—see if I could clear up some of the fog—or a nice glass of the Château Simard. If you open it up and let it hang around for an hour or so, even the recent years aren't so bad. Hal, the bartender, had picked up a bottle for me and hidden it behind the bar.

I drove toward home, but wine always wins. I ended up pulling my car into the alley behind the club and slipping in through the kitchen.

Marcia was working the grill. She used to wait tables at the Majestic, but she'd had dreams of being a chef, so Dally'd hired her to cook while she was getting her degree from cooking school, or whatever they called it. Somebody had ordered the mahimahi, which is marketingese for dolphin. But it's okay to eat it because it's the dolphin *fish,* not the dolphin *mammal.* It's just that calling it mahimahi makes it easier to distinguish from Flipper.

"Hey, Marcia."

She turned. "Oh, hey, Flap. Long time no see."

"It's only been three days."

She gave me a look you can only learn from waiting tables. "For you, that's a long time."

"Turn your fish over, sugar. It's done on that side."

She looked. "So it is. Thanks, sweetie."

She went back to work, I went into the club.

Dally was over by the stage, talking with Gwen Hughes about her nouveau swing-style band. I only overheard a little of the conversation, but it made me smile.

"So I told him," Gwen was explaining to Dally, "when you find me somebody alive today who can write a song as good as Strayhorn or Ellington or Fats Waller, *then* we'll do more original material. Until then shut the hell up. Besides, this stuff gets *everybody* dancing."

"Right."

Gwen nodded a final punctuation to her point and then continued setting up the stage. I'm certain that my face registered open admiration when she turned her red hair in my direction and smiled.

Dally started for the bar, saw me, and headed my way instead. "I thought you were going to call."

"I just came straight over, okay? Huyne didn't shoot me."

"I can see that." She patted my arm. "I'm happy."

"But he wanted to. He just got distracted."

We moved toward the bar. Dally knew what I needed. All she did was raise an eyebrow to Hal, and he moved like a dancer to get my bottle.

We sat.

"What makes you think he wanted to shoot you?"

"He was pointing his gun at me."

"Really?"

"With menace."

"I see." She wasn't upset. No need. I was alive and well. "And what distracted him?"

"The third body." A little drama on my part.

"Get the hell out!" Her eyes were wide.

"But get *this*. It was a dummy. A scarecrow, in fact."

What?" She pulled back from me a little.

"Uh-huh. And wait till you hear what the note said and what happened next."

Hal brought the bottle and two nice glasses, opened, smelled the cork himself, nodded, and set it down beside my glass.

"It's going to take about half an hour," he announced.

I grinned and shook my thumb in his direction. "Look who's Mr. Wine."

He rolled the toothpick in his mouth, looked down his nose at me, and winked with no expression whatsoever. "Learned from the master."

Dally was too impatient for any further male bonding to take place. "Third body?

"Was a dummy stuffed with newspaper. Here's the scene. Huyne is showing me some kind of odd finger-print anomalies in Beth Dane's file and then something about the third toxin—he's got these police files he's showing me—"

"Because?"

"He wanted to see how I'd react, I think. He expected me to act some way that would tip my hand to him, so to speak."

"But you disappointed him"—she leaned forward—"because you tip your hand to no man."

"Exactly. So then he gets all nervous and starts pointing his little snub-nose pistol at me—"

"Obviously not his official police piece."

"Exactly, again, and I think it's on his mind to shoot me in some important place, when all hell breaks loose on the other side of the park."

"Tenth Street?"

I shook my head. "Piedmont. Up by the Driving Club. It was staked out, but the cop up there was slow. Somebody pulled up—alone, by the way—ran over to the nearest lamp, tossed the dummy up so it hooked on the crook right by the light, and got back in the car in a matter of seconds, speeding away."

"Already I don't believe this."

"Of course, we don't know it's a dummy, so we run over expecting to see the third body, when one of its little feet falls off and we see it's not a real person at all. And guess what the note said?"

She leaned even closer. "It had a note, like the other ones?"

"Right. It said, 'Dance, Scarecrow.' "

"It said *what?*"

"Yeah." I was really enjoying her reaction. "And so I decide to beat it back here or go home and do my thing again, see what's up with *this*—"

"So you think your thing's working again?"

I shrugged. "Not like usual, but at least the power's not off entirely. So, anyway, I'm headed for my car when I see the bridge where I met Huyne—"

"Over by the bathhouse."

"And it's on *fire*. Or there's a fire over beside it."

"A fire?" Her shoulders sank, and I could see on her face that she was just about to connect the dots between the dummy and the fire.

"And Huyne's files and briefcase and everything is all burnt up."

" 'How about a little fire, Scarecrow?' " She was shaking her head

"I knew you'd get it."

"Well, of course I'd get it." She finally leaned back and absently reached for the bottle. "I've only seen *Wizard of Oz* about forty thousand times." She set the bottle down again, before she'd even poured, and stared at the floor. "But what's it about?"

"It's a message to somebody about something."

"It is?"

I nodded. "Isn't it? It's too much trouble and too dangerous for a prank, I think. And it's too—"

"Stupid?"

I nodded. "For anything else."

"It's like something a kid would do."

I grabbed the bottle away from her. "That's what Huyne said." I set the bottle down beside my other elbow. "We have to wait on this for a few more minutes."

"Okay," she said, completely distracted. "But who's the message from and who's it for, if you're right?"

"It's from the murderer." I was just throwing out idle guesses, really. "And it's to somebody who would find the body, like the police. Like Huyne."

"You're still suspecting him?"

"More than ever." I straightened up. "He wanted to shoot me. I suspect everyone who wants to shoot me."

"So where's Daniel all this time? You haven't mentioned him."

"Yeah." I nodded. "Where is he, I wonder?"

"He wasn't with you?"

"I called. No answer."

"You went to the park alone?" Her voice was getting a little sharper.

"The guy wasn't home. What was I supposed to do? And as long as we're on the subject of things that will rile you up, I couldn't find your tape recorder either, so I have no proof that Huyne threatened me."

"Damn it, Flap."

"Plus, I kidnapped the Lindbergh baby. What do you want from me? I was in a hurry. It all worked out fine. I'm here, I'm alive"—I looked at the bottle—"and I'm drinking this wine before it's been properly oxidized. Happy?" I poured without looking and plunked the bottle down in front of her for punctuation. Sometimes the best defense is a good drink.

She stared at me. She stared at the bottle. She poured, gulped, and took a deep breath.

"I'm finding you particularly exasperating lately, you know." She didn't look at me.

"I know, but I'm finding you particularly fascinating, so it all balances out."

"None of your smooth talk, mister." But she smiled, shaking her head.

"Now are you ready for the punch line?"

"There's more?" She finally looked me in the eye.

"Remember Dane was playing the bass in my little dream thing?"

"Right, shaped like a woman."

"What tune was he playing?"

She blinked. "You heard a tune?"

" 'Over the Rainbow.' "

"Get the *hell* out."

I held up my hand. "I wish I could, but I'm too far in."

"So what does it mean—the song?"

I leaned on the bar and picked up my glass, "It's got to mean that I know something that I don't *know* I know, doesn't it?"

"Nice sentence structure." She smiled into her wineglass. "Diction is so important."

"Still," I shrugger, "I've just got to get clear about a few things." Then: "Oh, my God."

"What?" She could see the look on my face.

"In Beth Dane's apartment." I closed my eyes, and

I could see it. "In the kitchen. There was a poster for the movie. It was like an old movie ad poster, with Dorothy's face and those three animal guys around her."

"Nice. One's a lion, one's a tin man, one's a scarecrow, and Dorothy's a human being. Earth, water, fire, and air—they represent, I believe, the elemental forces of this world, which is why they can suborn the metaphysics of the dreamworld."

I pulled back from her and tried to show my amazement. "What the hell have you been reading?"

"And furthermore, the elements are at war: tin man nearly rusted by water, scarecrow nearly destroyed by fire; the animal nature subverted in the natural environment—that is, the king of the animals terrified of his own nature. And in the center of it all, the human spirit, lost and searching for its center: home."

I took a long look at her face. She was absolutely delighted with herself, and I wondered for a second how long she'd been saving all that up. "Well, thank you, Mrs. Carl Jung, but all I had in mind was a kid who hated being a prostitute, dreaming of getting out of the life and into the beautiful land, which would have been *anywhere* but where she was."

"The two," she told me with a final flourish, "are not mutually exclusive."

"I guess not." I smiled and continued to stare at the lovely contour of her face. "And you must be pretty proud of yourself right about now."

"You don't have a copyright on the ersatz Jungian interpretation."

"Right." I agreed. "I can't even spell it. But where does all this get us?"

"Uh-huh." She nodded. "I'll tell you where this gets us. It gets us back to your little trick one last time."

"Third time's a charm."

"So they say." She sipped again. "So go."

She grabbed my wineglass away from me before I could take another sip.

I looked away. "I guess it's kind of got me . . . unsettled, this thing of not being able to make the trick work like I want it to."

"So get right back on it." She forged ahead. "That's the difference between you and people who lead lives of quiet desperation. The desperate types either try something and give up or at least back off when it doesn't work. On the other hand, the pig-headed types of this world—"

"Of which we find an abundance—"

"They bump their heads time after time on the same obstacle, doggedly not giving up but making the same stupid play over and over again."

"Which is just as bad?"

"According to my reckoning, yes. You, on the final hand, try something, but then if it doesn't work, you back off, think about it, and try something *else*. Something different. You don't give up, but you don't beat a dead horse."

" 'Don't pull punches/don't push the river.' " I nodded. "To quote St. Van."

"Van Morrison doesn't enter into it today. He already admitted he doesn't know what enlightenment is." She was full speed ahead. "You've got to scuttle on back to your digs and uncover the gold." She finished the wine in my glass. "And you have to keep a clear head to do it too."

"You can't be serious."

"As a crutch. Now git, as my mother used to tell me when I was someplace I wasn't supposed to be."

"I'm not supposed to be here with you?"

"Right." She stood and started shooing me off the barstool. "That's right. I'll finish this bottle of wine for you; it'll be partial payment for my bathroom door. And by the way, here's something to factor in: Ray Bolger, who played the part of the Scarecrow, was better known as a hoofer. So put that in your pipe. Now you go do your work. Go on."

"But . . ."

"Now!"

She had spoken and turned heads doing it. Hal, for one, was staring, a little more amused than I would have liked personally. Gwen was visibly trying not to laugh, unwinding her microphone cord. Marcia had come to the kitchen door and was peering out.

I straightened my coat, mostly for dignity's sake, nodded a cordial, if curt, adieu to all and sundry, and slipped quietly out of the club, as the band started their sound check.

29

MOONLIGHT

The apartment was dark. The moon was coming up. The streets were relatively quiet. I was staring out the porch windows. Glass on three sides, in the daylight you call it a sunporch, but now the moonlight was spilling in, making everything look as quiet as it sounded. It was a visual hush, a silver sigh.

Maybe it was Dally's brief tirade about the mythological nature of Frank Baum's writing, but I had it in my head that what I needed to do was sink into the Universal Unconscious, like swimming in the sea. That's all. Just swim.

Silver and shadow and the clicking of the bare tree limbs in the cold air made a nice hypnotic blanket, and it wasn't long before I was halfway into dreamland.

All at once I was talking to Mickey "the Pineapple" Nichols. He was staring at me across a table that was shaped like a lake and made out of water.

"The Internet is to our intellectual life what the Universal Unconscious is to our psychological life. In fact the Internet *is* the new Universal Unconscious. It is not even a metaphor any longer."

Then we turned, because there was tango music down a long corridor. In the shadows, as I had once before, I saw a girl crawl out of a picture, disappear down the hall into the shadows, return a moment later with another, smaller picture, and hang it in place of the original, tossing away the empty frame.

Then I saw Joepye Adder switching frames up and down the hall, like a three-card monte player. But the hall was filled with trees, like in Piedmont Park, and Joe was sitting on a little box in the woods and drinking wine. There was dance music in the background, like a movie sound track.

When it was all over, Mick turned back to me, smiled, pulled out his piece, and said, "Whelp. Closing time."

Then—with a really earsplitting crack—he shot me in the heart.

Boom. I was wrenched from my vision the way you wake up from a dream sometimes: bolt upright, heart pounding, checking to see if what happened in the dream really happened to you.

No blood on my chest, so I assumed for the moment that I hadn't been shot. Still, the pistol fire was ringing in my ears, and I felt a pain in my rib cage. I couldn't remember how many years it had been since I'd given up cigarettes, but I knew I would have smoked one then if I'd had any in the house.

I just sat in the canvas director's chair on the porch staring out at the moon on the street for maybe half an hour. I was shaken partly because of the combined intensity and brevity of my little vision and partly because of the crystal reality of Mickey's gunshot.

By the time my heart was back to normal and the craving for a smoke had gone, I knew everything. It was straight in my mind. Not the answers exactly, but all the right questions.

30

WIRED

"Who do we know that can really do something with a computer? I mean, the spooky stuff."

"Flap?" Dally's voice was odd.

"Yes. Who did you think it was?"

"You sound"—she seemed worried—"different."

"I am different. I thought it was one of the things you liked about me."

"Flap . . ."

"I did the thing, and I know the score. So who knows computers?"

"You already did your thing?" She was still a beat behind. It was my fault.

"Look," I started, a little impatiently, "I'll explain it all in a minute, but I don't want to lose the momentum I've got now, okay? It's like I got electroshock or something. I'm buzzed."

"Okay, okay." She was trying to catch up. "How about Dirt Gainer?"

"Who?"

"Remember the cop who followed you home the other night when you got shot at? That kid. He's a whiz, they say."

"That cop? His name is Dirt?"

"Short for Dirt Bike, he loves dirt bikes. His given name is Gyles. And he's on nights this week, obviously."

"He's a computer whiz?" I shook my head. "Why do I find this hard to believe? He's just a kid."

"Who do you think it is that knows computers these days, pal? They're all kids."

"Okay." I shrugged. "How do I get him to help me look something up?"

"You can't." I could hear her smile. "But I can. Pick you up in five."

We met at the front of the Midtown Station, and Dirt was standing in the doorway.

"Hey, Ms. Oglethorpe." He was smiling ear to ear. "It's a honor." He stuck out his hand; she shook it.

"Hey, Mr. Tucker." A big smile and a shake to me too. "Now what can I do exactly? Ms. Oglethorpe was kind of sketchy on the phone."

Once inside the little building, we moved right away to some sort of special computer lab, not to the kid's desk. All Dally had told him on the phone was that we needed to do some first-class snooping, and he'd said he would help in any *legal* way he could. She told me he'd stressed the word. She seemed to admire it. Just made him seem young to me.

In the lab he sat at one of the keyboards; Dally and I flanked him.

"Could you look up Irgo Winfred Dane?"

"Who?" He turned my way.

"He's a musician, plays bass for the symphony and the opera, also jazz. Just type in 'Dane.'"

"Naw." He smiled. "You do that and you'd get three hundred million matches. See, anything at all with the word *Dane* in it would be a match."

Dally squinted at the screen. "You mean there could be, like, a thousand references to people in Denmark?"

He nodded. "Probably more."

"So we have to be more specific." I leaned back. "How about, Irgo Winfred Dane the bass player?"

"Well, see"—he shook his head—"you could end up with a million references to bass players and still be looking at half of Denmark. That's why I think we should just try looking up his E-mail address in the old electronic phone book."

"You can do that?" I suddenly felt myself alive in an age of miracles.

"Here it is," he said, almost to himself. "HWDBass at south dot net." Then he turned to me. "Now, what are you really looking for?"

I stared at the screen distractedly. "I honestly don't know. But there's something not right about the guy,

I've really got that in my head. I've been told several times how strange he is. I'd like to know what that means."

He nodded. "The problem is, these search engines, they just love specificity."

I looked over at him. "I want to know if Dane is into anything weird on the computer, on the Net. How about that?"

He nodded. "That would all be coded probably. You mean, like drugs or stolen items or pornography?"

"You can get all that on the Internet?" I looked at his profile.

Dally peered over at me. "You really *do* live in another time zone, don't you, pal? At least read *Time* magazine every once in a while. Even if you don't have a computer, they'll tell you what's going on in the cyber world."

"As it happens," I told her, with a great amount of specificity, "I don't want any part of the so-called cyber world. Thanks, but no thanks. I've got my hands full with my own little world."

Officer Gainer cleared his throat. "How about," he said, not looking at either one of us, "if I try a few things and you all go get some coffee or something?" Then he looked at me. "This is about those two hanging girls, ain't it?"

I nodded. It was a good guess on his part, and I was once again adjusting my attitude about the kid.

He smiled grimly. "Good. I surely would like to help out on that one."

"Where're you from, Officer Gainer?" I smiled back. "If you don't mind my asking."

"Shoot, I don't mind at all. I'm from Jasper. It's way south. Why do you ask?"

"Well, Dally and I were born down that way too. Not Jasper, but definitely South Georgia. I just thought I recognized something familiar in your accent, that's all."

"Is that right?" He lit up even more. "Whereabouts you all from?"

"I hate to be the one," Dally interrupted, "but let's do a little work, and save this for later, could we?"

"Oh," he nodded, "sure thing." He wasn't the least bit put off. "Here we go." And he started typing things into the computer right away.

Dally and I headed for the coffee.

Just a couple of blocks up the street was a fancy Italian place where I'd had lunch a couple of times in the presence of one William Fred Scott, artistic director of the Atlanta Opera. Fred was one of those guys some people found intimidating: "That Fred Scott, he thinks he knows everything." But the irrefutable fact was he actually *did* know everything, so I always enjoyed our little lunches. When Fred showed up in the doorway of the place, you'd have thought the pope had come in.

"Maestro! It's so good to see you! Quickly. Our best table for the maestro and his friend."

Ever since then they'd been very cordial to me, the maestro's friend. Fame by association. It's what allowed Dally and me to have a table, order up some thick espresso, and stare out the window talking without being bothered by a lot of "What *else* will you be ordering this evening?"

"They treat you well here." Dally smiled when we were seated.

"This is where Fred and I come for lunch sometimes."

"I see." She looked at the tablecloth. "Funny your mentioning Fred, what with Dane's being associated with the opera and all."

I knew what she was trying to do. She was trying to vex me with coincidentals so that I would spill my whole story to her. But for just this once, because everything else about it was so odd, I'd decided to play it a little close to the vest, as they say.

"Yeah." I watched the waiter hurry back with our espresso. "Fred loves this place." I turned to her. "You should try the risotto sometime."

"Okay." She slumped a little. "So you'll tell me what you want to when you want to—I get it."

"I'm not trying to hide anything." I softened a little. "It's just that everything I have in mind at the moment is so out of the ordinary."

"How do you mean, if *that's* okay to ask?"

"I mean . . ." I waited while the waiter set down the cups and asked if there was anything else he could do for us at the moment. He turned the saucers, offered us our napkins, and straightened the tablecloth before he left.

"Fred must really make an impression on these guys." She watched him retreat.

"He makes an impression on everybody, don't you think?"

"So you were saying . . ." she prompted.

"That this is all out of the realm of how this ordinarily happens for me. I mean, how many times have I told you that it's just a question of seeing the big picture, finding things stuck in your head you'd forgotten were there—that sort of thing?"

"Okay, about a million."

"Right." I nodded and sipped my brew. "But this feels different."

"How?"

I leaned forward. "What if Mickey really shot me and all this since that night has been a deathbed hallucination? You see that sort of thing in movies all the time."

She rolled her eyes. "Not that again. Haven't we already been over all—I'm not even talking about that with you, Flap."

"I woke up from my little dream thing convinced that Mick shot me."

"Shot you?"

"Yeah." I sipped again. "Just now, just earlier. I was shaking from it for half an hour before I could call you."

She stared at me. "Well, I can explain that . . . if you want me to."

"Oh, really?" I think even the waiter heard my skepticism, and he was fifty feet away.

"Yes, really." She plunged ahead. "You've got yourself a time bomb."

That stopped me.

"See"—she leaned on her elbows—"when Mick tried to kill you, you had to be tough. Probably gave him the 'bullets bounce off me' speech."

I laughed. She'd heard parts of the speech on several previous occasions.

"So you think you're calm," she continued, "but then he actually pulls the trigger and shoots the gun, and your body has a chemical reaction. Can't help it. Fear is biochemical. Only you've suppressed it. You've ignored it. This little panic you've got going in your subconscious—which you wade around in while you're doing your little trick, see?—it's just waiting there for you, going 'Hi, remember me?' when you bump into it."

" 'Hi, remember me?' "

"Along those lines." She sipped delicately from her cup.

"What the *hell* have you been reading?"

"Just trying to keep up with you." She smiled sweetly. "That's all."

"So my suppressed fear is a time bomb that goes off when I least expect it because I haven't dealt with my panic from the other night." I looked at her. "Do you know how much I hate Freudian analysis?"

"Actually"—she gave me the big shrug—"I'm reading D. H. Lawrence, if you must know. I'm only inferring Freud."

"From Lawrence? It's not that big a leap."

"So you see my point?"

"No." I was getting irritated, for some reason. "I don't see your point at all. You're just trying to get me to tell you what's going on, and for once I don't feel like it."

"Repression." She said it just to make me mad, and I knew it.

So instead of blowing my top, which would have been the cowboy way, I took a moment of reflection instead.

Why exactly didn't I want to tell Dally everything about this? I considered the big three reasons men do anything: hunger, fear, sex.

Hunger we could eliminate right away, because I was always hungry, so that was a constant. Constants are not, by definition, variables: ipso facto. Sex was a subject Dally and I had danced around for most of our lives. I'd been married, she'd had boyfriends, we were generally all right about it. Still, I had sensed a little jealousy from her concerning the dearly departed Janey Finster. And I knew I'd had a monkey brain– territorial moment myself concerning Huyne's atten-tion to Dalliance. So maybe something was coming to the surface there too. But *fear*—there's something to really mess you up. Fear motivates without seeming to; fear is the unseen mover; fear wages war behind many a mask—to paraphrase, among others, old Joe Campbell.

But it wasn't, as Dally had begun to formulate, a fear of death. Death was not the thing. Death's okay by me: stepping, at last, through the golden curtain and into the brighter reality. Something to look forward to, really.

Still, I was afraid of something. Sitting there considering it, I had a moment to feel the flint, notice the numbness from the rush of adrenaline.

"Hey." Her voice seemed to be coming to me from a million miles away. "What's the deal? Where are you?"

"You're right."

"I love being right." She smiled. "About what?"

"Something's got me spooked. That's my problem."

"I see." She finished her espresso. "Like what?"

"I don't know. But it's—I'm not used to it, this feeling."

"Doesn't happen to you very often. What exactly are you afraid of, I mean in general?"

"Bad wine, the wrong kind of work, and truck drivers who fall asleep at the wheel beside me on the highway." I finished my espresso and plunked a ten on the table—about the same time I finished my introspection loop apparently. I'd just have to deal with the fear a little later. "Let's get back to the station house and see what the kid's scared up."

"To coin a phrase," she told me, standing up.

Dirt Gainer was staring at the computer screen when we came into the lab. He didn't even look our way when he spoke to us.

"Y'all ain't *about* to believe this." He took a deep, shaky breath and leaned back.

We came over and looked. On the screen was a very clear photograph of a young girl, topless, dressed like a cheerleader only holding her skirt up so you could see her underpants, and crying. She looked vaguely familiar.

"What the hell is this?" Dally whispered.

"That," the kid said even softer than Dally, still staring at the screen, "is the late Beth Dane."

"Beth Dane?" I stared. It was like seeing a ghost.

"That's right," the kid said, transfixed. "And here's the worst part . . ." He finally looked up at me and Dally, with an expression that was all but begging for some kind of explanation. "This is a Web site that's designed by Irgo Winfred Dane." Then he looked back at the screen, baffled. "Her uncle."

31

DANCING FOOTPRINTS

We stared at the screen for another minute before he spoke up again. "The rest of the pictures—they're lots worse than this."

Dally patted him on the shoulder, staring at the photo. "If it makes you feel any better, the crying is fake. Staged."

"What?" He looked up at her.

"She's wearing tons of cheap mascara, but it's not running. Also, the rims of her eyes aren't the least bit red, and, finally, don't the rills seem kind of thick?"

"Glycerine," I confirmed. "Movie tears."

"Really?" He looked back at the screen. "You think?"

I nodded. "Doesn't make it any less troublesome,

but yeah. I mean, look at her expression. Isn't it a little
. . . exaggerated?"

"I guess." He was staring at it.

But we all knew we were trying just a little too
hard to distance ourselves from the image.

"How'd you come up with this?" I looked at the
kid.

"Oh," he said, "I went to the Web master part, and
then you do this and you do that and I traced the
account to the server and it was the same account as
the E-mail address we found, which I dialed up and
it's the guy, so—"

Dally sat down. "So she wasn't just trying to get
out of the life, as you were saying. She was trying to
get away from this? From her uncle?"

I found I had to take a seat too. "This is all a little
too much to swallow at the moment." I looked at her.
"I've admired this guy for a good many years. I mean,
he plays *jazz,* for God's sake."

"Your argument being"—she looked at me from
beneath arched eyebrows—"that depravity and good
taste don't go hand in hand? Ever hear of a little
French aristocrat name of de Sade?"

"Yeah." I nodded. "I hear he really knew how to
decorate a room, but Dane is . . . I just have to adjust my opinion of the guy, and it's going to take a
minute, okay?"

"Okay." And she left it alone.

Officer Gainer looked at me. "What does this do to
our case?"

I folded my arms. "I guess it could actually further the cause of the difficult-to-believe suicide scenario."

"Or it could make Dane a very bad man indeed," Dally said.

I turned to her. "As in like, *he* killed her? Because she wanted out . . . of some kind of life he had a part in?"

"Isn't it possible?" She stared right back at me.

I took a quick look at the screen, then back at Dally. "I guess anything is possible, huh?"

"Anything." She meant it.

The kid finally shook his head, like he was trying to clear it. "Y'all mind if I just get out of this site? I don't have to shut it off entirely, but can I take this photo off the screen at least?"

"Absolutely." Dally and I jumped at the same time.

Then, from behind us: "This is an interesting party."

I didn't even have to turn around. I recognized Huyne's voice.

"Detective." I nodded but didn't look.

"What's going on here?" He'd addressed the question more to Officer Gainer.

"Helping out Ms. Oglethorpe," he said right back. "She's always so good to us I figured . . . you know . . ."

Huyne was in the room. "I know." He smiled at Dally. She smiled back. Then he sat down at the table with us. "Looked like Beth Dane on the screen a little."

"It was." I finally looked at him.

"How'd you find that picture?"

"Mr. Tucker had an idea." The kid began, then trailed off.

Huyne looked at me hard. "Yeah, he's full of ideas."

"In this case"—I stared right back—"I got the idea to look into Dane's involvement with anything on the Internet. This is one of the things we came up with."

That shut him up for a second. His eyes got bigger, and his chin jutted forward for half a second, but he was cool.

"Dane's got a site that features his niece half dressed?"

We all stared at the picture the kid hadn't had a chance to cut off.

Dally nodded. "That's what it looks like."

"There's other pictures here too." The kid spoke up.

Huyne stared at the screen. "Can you copy this or save it all somehow and give me a disk?"

The kid nodded.

"Also"—Huyne went on—"a report involving what other links are involved, how the site is connected, I mean exactly, with Dane. What—" He looked at the officer. "I'm assuming he used some kind of coding to hide himself?"

"Yes, sir."

"Then also include in your report what coding and so forth, right?"

"Yes, sir."

Dally patted the kid's arm. "Sorry. Looks like I got you in paperwork hell."

He smiled at her. "Shoot. This is great. I get my name on the case." He looked at Huyne. "I discovered key evidence."

Huyne folded his arms. "I thought Mr. Tucker—"

"I only had an *idea*, remember?" I smiled. "Officer Gainer here actually discovered the evidence. I was out getting coffee at the time."

He took only a second to think about it. "Okay, Officer Gainer. You discovered key evidence in this case, and it's duly noted."

"Thank you, sir." But he smiled at Dally, not at the detective.

Huyne turned to Dalliance. "Anyway, I've been looking for you." Shot a glance to me. "You too." Back to Dally. "I went to your club, which is where Tucker told me he was going—"

"Which is where he *did* go first," she told him, "but I made him go home to do a little work."

"Work?" He made it sound like he couldn't believe I'd ever done anything like work.

"He had to cogitate," she said simply.

"Ah," Huyne shot back, in something of a wry fashion. "By which you mean he sat around his digs performing his hocus-pocus all over the place."

"I'll thank you to watch that *pocus* talk in mixed company, pal." I stood. I was in no mood to be in the same room with Huyne at that point. "Now the fact is, I actually do have work to do, however difficult it may be for you to believe, and I'd like to be on my way. So if you will excuse me and Ms. Oglethorpe—"

She stood too, on cue. "I'm his chauffeur."

"Don't you want to hear what else we found in the park?"

He knew that would stop both of us.

He paused, just for the sake of theatre, and then went on, not looking at either of us. "We found footprints in the embankment under the bridge that we're pretty certain belong to Joe Adder."

"How would you begin to find that out already?" I had to know.

"Didn't you ever notice that he had that duct tape on one of his boots?" He looked at Dally. "Joe wears army surplus paratrooper boots most of the winter, but one has a thin sole so he's wrapped duct tape around it. Makes a very distinctive footprint."

"I'd imagine." She nodded.

"You never noticed that about him?" He looked my way.

"I've already told you once this evening that you win in the print identification competition. Goes for fingers and feet both."

"Maybe your vaunted powers of deduction aren't all they're cracked up to be."

"Vaunted?" I think I managed an ironic twist of the mouth. "I wouldn't know about that. Sometimes it just works, and sometimes it doesn't. Sometimes the angel kisses you, and sometimes she doesn't."

He ignored me. "So, the thing is, I've just about set

my mind on him. He's the murderer. Shouldn't be hard to gather up."

"So who's his helper?" I started moving for the door.

"Hmm?" He was momentarily distracted by our movement, I thought.

"Who was with him tonight or, you know, in on this thing with him tonight?"

"What do you mean?"

I stopped in the doorway and turned slowly. "While Joe was setting fire to your little campsite, who was tossing the dummy up the lamppost? No matter how you drive, I don't think you can get from the Piedmont side of the park all the way around to the bridge where your stuff was hidden, set a fire, and disappear again in the time frame in question."

His mouth formed a word, but it never made it into the sound dimension. I could see he was thinking, trying not to come up with the same conclusion as I'd just presented.

"You've got to drive down Piedmont, right on Monroe." He was tracing the path in his mind's eye. "Then you turn in there at that little street. If there's no traffic and the lights are with you, it's got to take . . . say, seven minutes to drive around to where the bridge is. You don't think we spent that much time over on the Piedmont side of the park?"

"Longer, but you don't just run up, start a match, and beat it. He had to gather up your stuff and douse it and—besides, how did he even know you were there? He had to be watching you, don't you think?" I nodded. "That's my theory. Joe was hidden down the ravine north of the bridge, because that's where he camps a lot of the time anyway, and he was watching you, and when we left, he just walked up and started with the pyrotechnics. Somebody else tossed the dummy."

"And do you have a theory about that as well?" He folded his arms and held his ground.

"As a matter of fact, I do." I took one more look at the title of Dane's Web site, then offered Dally my arm, and we started out the door. "But we're leaving now."

I could see that he was thinking about coming after us, but he wanted to stay cool in Dally's presence, so he just smiled and let us leave.

But finally he couldn't resist. He called out after us, "Well? What *is* your theory?"

Now, I wasn't about to say anything else to him, but just as we hit the door into the waiting room of the station house, I heard the kid's voice.

"He thinks it's Dane."

When we opened the door to the station house, we were hit with a knifelike jab of the coldest air I could remember in January. But it wasn't as cold as the name we'd seen on Dane's pornographic Web site. It was called "The Little Dancers."

32

SINGLE-BULLET THEORY

As we made it to Dally's car, she looked down the dark streets in front of the station house.

"I've got this image," she started, "of Dane and Joepye, like they're Frankenstein and Igor, trundling down the street, body snatcher style."

"And this troubles you."

She nodded, getting her keys ready. "It's like I'm not taking all this seriously enough, you know?"

"Or," I told her as she unlocked my door, "maybe it's just a little psychological insulation—in keeping with your current interest in such things."

She moved to the driver's side. "Sorry?"

"You're hoping that an image like that will distance you from the actual events. You're trying to keep the harsher truth at bay."

"Could be."

We got in. She cranked the car, then turned my way. "So where to? I'm assuming we're not through."

"Right. But I think I'll have this all wrapped up tonight."

"Tonight?" She apparently couldn't help the incredulity.

"At least the murders of Beth Dane and Minnie," I nodded. "I'm hoping that Dane and Joe are over at Dane's right now." She pulled out into the street. "I'd like to speak with them."

"You obviously think they killed the girls." She headed toward the park. "And I'm not saying I don't agree." Still, she set her head at an odd angle. "Beth I get, in a way—she was maybe part of some weird ring of prostitutes and Internet stuff or something—but why Minnie? And why the spooky hanging thing?"

"That's what I want to speak with them about."

She drove a little faster. "Are we worried about confronting the monster in its lair?"

I smiled at her. "I think you could kick Dane all over town if you wanted to. And Joepye gets confused about which foot to walk with, so . . ."

"Still, you wouldn't like to call up Daniel now, see if he's busy?"

"Please"—I shifted in my seat—"one problem at a time. If I call Daniel, he's going to tell Foggy, who will only want to know what I'm doing about Janey—"

"Which, at the moment, is bupkis."

"Exactly." I nodded. "So let's just include them out at the moment, okay?"

"Like you said," she affirmed, "one crime at a time."

The night seemed blacker than usual, and the moon had gone behind some charcoal clouds. The cold and the humidity made the streetlights churn out steam like a cheap fog machine. It wasn't late, but the streets were empty.

Dally clicked on the radio hoping for some cheery music and got a weather report instead: chance of an ice storm.

We pulled up across the street from Dane's big old house, killed the engine, and sat in the car a moment.

"This wants a little caution, at least," I told Dally, staring at the house. "My plan is to go around back first, peer in a couple of windows."

"While I do what?" She was already shivering. The car heater hadn't even had a chance to warm up, and now it was off again.

I turned in her direction. "There's probably no sending you off to your nice warm nightclub."

"Not really," she told me languidly. "Band hasn't started yet."

I glanced at my watch. She was right. It wasn't even nine o'clock. Seemed like midnight.

"So, cover me." I smiled. "I'll come back around front in a minute, and we'll just go in for a nice visit. If you see anything that looks like trouble, blast the horn."

"Can do," she finally agreed. "But don't take forever. I'm freezing."

"I'll hurry," I told her, and braced myself for the air.

I shot across the street, avoiding the brightest part of the streetlight. I rounded the house. The only lights besides the porch light came from several upstairs rooms.

I shot a glance into a few side windows, but it was too dark to see inside.

I made it to the backyard, and I was about to peek in the kitchen, where there was a little night-light or something, when I heard a thumping noise come from the direction of the gazebo.

I dropped low, spun around, and tried to adjust my eyes to the wet black night.

Somebody was kicking something in the gazebo. I tried not to let my mind get carried away, but images of dead bodies—or worse not *quite* dead bodies—getting booted around sort of drifted into my inner eye.

I stayed low, kept close to some bushes, and got to a place where I could see into the interior of the gazebo.

There, lashed to the banister with duct tape, was Joepye Adder. He was looking right at me and kicking the hell out of the floor. His eyes were wild. His mouth was covered with more of the silver duct tape, and his breathing was labored.

I checked very carefully around the whole yard but finally gave up. There could have been twenty guys hiding in twice as many dark places. I just took a deep breath, stood up, and moved as calmly as I could toward the poor guy.

First order of business was to get the tape off his mouth. He was really having a hard time breathing through his thick red nose.

"Ack!"

Honest to God, that's what he said, and it was really loud.

Then he lowered his voice. "Flap."

"Hey, bud. What are you doing?"

"Oh"—he was catching his breath—"nothing much. Could you get my arms aloose? I got a cramp or a charley horse something fierce."

"How long you been out in this cold night air?"

He looked around like he could see how cold the air was. "Not long. But you know, in my condition . . ." He left the rest of the sentence to my imagination.

"Who left you here like this, Joe?"

"Mr. Dane. But he didn't mean a thing by it. He was just making sure I didn't wander off to get a drink. I'd have done it too. I really need a drink."

I had taken out my keys and was using one of the jagged edges to saw the duct tape. I got one arm free.

"You know"—I looked at his face, gray and smeared—"I saw you in the park awhile ago." *Why not give it a try?* I thought.

"Yeah." He was watching me work on the tape. "That Detective Huyne sure is mean."

"Pointed a gun at me."

He looked up at my face then. "Yeah. You know, he's done that to me too."

"That why you set his stuff on fire?"

"Naw," he said, then looked at me. "W-what are you talking about?"

"Is Dane inside?"

He looked up at one of the windows on the second floor, the only one in back that was lit up.

I had just gotten Joe's other arm freed when the night was ripped apart by a long, loud blast from Dally's car horn.

I jumped off the gazebo and was halfway around the house before I heard heavy footsteps on Dane's front porch. I was all the way around to the front yard when I saw Dane running, as best he could, for his Mercedes in the driveway.

Dally was nearly across the street, yelling at Dane to stop.

I was yelling at Dally to get down, because Dane had a hunting rifle pointed right at her.

"So." She turned my way for a second, her face set in a hard smile, and hollered out, "You don't think that maybe one little bullet could bounce off me too?"

Before I could even think what to say, the gun erupted. Lightning shot out of the barrel, there was a metallic crunching noise, and Dally went down in the street.

I flew through the air, wrestled the gun away from Dane, and bashed his forehead as hard as I could with the butt of the rifle. I hoped I hit him hard enough to kill him.

33

SMOKING GUN

I was in the street kneeling next to Dalliance before the gun on the ground had even stopped smoking.

"Hi." She stared up at me. "Come here often?"

"You're okay?"

"He missed me by a mile, didn't you see where he was pointing that thing?"

"All I saw"—I stared down at her—"was that it was pointed at you."

"In my general direction, maybe." She managed to sit up, then turned to her car. "But take a gander at my rear fender."

It had a new hole in it, and the tire was hissing.

Dane groaned.

I stood, helped Dally up, and we both took the ten

or so steps to Dane's side. I pointed the rifle down at him, but it wasn't really necessary.

"My head." He was clutching his temples like he was trying to make sure nothing would fall off.

"Why don't you just lie right there, Mr. Dane?"

He squinted up at me. "Mr. Tucker? Is that you?"

"Yes."

He looked over at Dally. "You're all right. Thank God. That damned rifle."

"What?" Dally shifted her weight to one leg.

"I was certain I had it pointed to the ground, but you startled me." He was still holding his head. "Did I shoot myself?"

"No," I told him. "I whacked you in the head."

"You did?" He was still trying to focus on my face. "Why?"

"Because you shot at Ms. Oglethorpe."

"The gun went off. I didn't shoot . . . my God, you don't think I'd shoot at . . . what did you hit me with? A brick? A truck?"

"Your gun."

"I think I need to go to the hospital." He was trying to sit up.

"I think"—I knelt beside him and spoke directly to his face—"you'll just be going to the police. Your head's okay." I got closer and whispered, "You're lucky I didn't kill you, you son of a bitch. You ever point so much as a *finger* at Dalliance again, and that'll be your last second on this earth. I promise."

"Ohh," he moaned, squeezing his head between

his hands. "Could you please stop shouting? And why do you have to be so angry with me? I told you I didn't *mean* for the gun to go off—"

"Shut up." I interrupted. "You pimp your own niece, then kill her because she wants out, and you throw in some poor art student who never did you any harm at all. You are one sick cargo, and I'm sorry I ever thought anything good about you."

Dally laid her hand on my arm. "Easy there, big fella."

"What are you talking about?" Dane's eyes were wild, and he struggled to get up. "I don't know what makes you think I could kill my niece, but you couldn't be more mistaken. I loved her. She was *family,* for God's sake."

I didn't offer to help him up. "You're saying you didn't have a Web site with her photographs?"

He let the question hang there for a long moment. Then: "You know about that." He finally made it to a standing position, took a step back as if he were about to fall down again, then steadied himself. "That's what I was doing upstairs when I heard the noise down here."

Dally and I looked at each other, then back at Dane.

He blinked. "I was purging everything from my hard drive. I didn't want any embarrassing questions when I took Adder to the police."

My turn to blink. "You were taking Joepye to the police?"

He nodded. "I have to sit down."

He stumbled to the front porch steps. We followed.

"I've got him tied up out back. I had to keep him here while I took care of my computer. *He* killed Beth. And that other poor girl."

"All by himself?" I tried to fill the phrase with as much skepticism as possible under the circumstances.

"Yes. He did it to scare me." He looked up at me, white as the moon. "It worked too." He closed his eyes. "He killed Beth and then tried to blackmail me about the . . . the Web site."

"He knew about the—" I began.

"I don't know how," Dane interrupted, "but he knew all the details. When you told me he'd been an electrical engineer at Tech, it made more sense. That's part of the real reason I hired you in the first place, to find out what really happened, get some real information about Adder. Still, I don't know how a person in his current condition would even have access to a computer."

"Well"—I took in a deep breath—"assuming I buy any of this, which is a big assumption to begin with, I could tell you that Joepye has odd jobs all over. He cleans up at the Midtown post office. He does small handyman jobs sometimes in business offices. And he visits the police station on a regular basis. Everyone takes him for granted. He might have computer access at any one of those places."

"But how would he ever know about my site?"

Dane held his temples. "It didn't make sense to me. It's very well hidden. Still. He came to me the night you and he found Beth's body, told me he'd killed her, and wanted money to keep quiet about the . . . site."

"Joepye Adder," Dally threw in, "told you he killed Beth Dane?"

"Yes."

"And you believed him?" I shook my head.

"The more he talked over the days, the more it was obvious he knew all about Beth's death . . . and then the other murder . . . murders. Did you know, for example, that the girls were killed with toxins stolen from the CDC before they were hanged?"

"He told you that?" Dally shot me a look.

Dane nodded. "And he told me some wild story about a French surrealist who'd killed himself in the same way the girls were killed—or seemed to be killed, I suppose. What was that all about?" He closed his eyes. "I think I'm going to pass out." He leaned over and put his head between his legs. "Go ask him. He's out back in the gazebo."

"Um . . . I hope he is." I looked at Dally. "I might have turned him loose."

Dane looked up, stunned. "What?"

"He told me you'd tied him up back there. What was I supposed to think?" I took Dane's arm and started around the house to the backyard. "Come on. Let's have a look."

He made an awful noise standing up, and I nearly

had to drag him around the house. By the time we made it to the spot where I'd found Joepye only moments earlier, Dane was completely winded. And there was nothing in the gazebo but a lot of torn-up duct tape.

34

GHOST DANCER

Back in the house, we called the Midtown station house right away and found Huyne still there. Dally talked to him, told him where we were, and why we were there, and what Dane had told us, all in about three well-chosen sentences. It was very elegant.

He must have left the place before she'd hung up the phone because I'd swear he was pulling up in the street out front inside of five minutes.

I met him on the porch. "I left the gun, the one that Dane used to shoot at Ms. Oglethorpe, in the front yard there. It's got my prints on the barrel housing, but not the stock or the trigger." I nodded at it with my head. "Dally can fill you in on the rest."

Two officers moved past us in the shadows on the

porch and into the living room, where Dane was lying on the sofa, a cold towel on his head.

"Where do you think you're going?" Huyne stood to block my way off the porch.

"Look," I told him tersely, "I think I know where Joe went. He went to his home base. It's not that far from where you were staked out, under the bridge in the park. I let him loose. Maybe he is what Dane says he is, or maybe he's just a little goofball like I say. Whichever. I have to go get him. You can see that."

"He's a suspect in a very big murder case." Huyne shook his head. "This is a police matter."

I ground my teeth. "Okay, then send one of those uniforms with me, and they can do the driving. They can arrest him. Call me an informant. I'll take the nice policeman to a place where he can find the suspect. Okay?"

He could see how tightly wound I was. He only took a second to consider what to do.

"Gainer!"

That almost made me smile.

Officer Gainer appeared in the doorway. "Yes, sir?"

"Would you please take Mr. Tucker here over to the park? He thinks he might be able to tell you where to apprehend a suspect." He looked at me. "If this all works out the way Ms. Oglethorpe described it to me on the phone . . . and you really do get Adder—some of which I still doubt—but I say *if* this is righteous . . . this actually could be the beginning of a beautiful friendship . . . Louis."

"Hey, Mr. Tucker." The kid lit up.

I smiled at Huyne. "So, you did get that after all. And by the way, I know that you're only doing this so that you can be alone with Ms. Oglethorpe."

"That's right." Huyne smiled back. "Alone with her—and Dane, and the other officers—"

"But *I* won't be here." I nodded.

"I'll see her home. Time to go now," Huyne told Gainer, still smiling. "Watch out for Mr. Tucker, hear?"

I didn't know if he meant the kid was supposed to look after me or to make sure I didn't do anything wrong.

I don't think Gainer even heard it. He practically shot past me. I took one last look into the living room where Dally was talking to the other officer, then shoved off the porch toward the waiting prowler.

By the time we'd made it into the park the back way, I'd filled the kid in on the strange details.

"You don't think that Joepye Adder could actually have been blackmailing Mr. Dane."

I shook my head. "No, I don't. I still maintain that Joepye couldn't blackmail a doughnut out of the counter help at Krispy Kreme. Still, the little guy's involved in this thing some way, don't you think?"

"I guess," he told me, but he obviously didn't mean it.

He'd turned off the lights a block away from the park entrance, shut off the engine, and coasted to a stop. We got out of the car and barely closed the doors. He checked his gun.

The air was cold and heavy as lead.

As we got to the edge of the park, I began to feel little needles stinging my face and hands.

"Ice storm," the kid whispered. "They said it was coming."

He followed me on around the perimeter of the woods until we were at the edge of an embankment about twenty yards north of the bridge where the fire had been earlier in the evening. In just the time it had taken us to make it there, the trees were already frosted, and the distinctive sound of sleet was clinking on the limbs and the ground all around us. When you looked out at the streetlamps, you could see a billion little white dots drifting almost silently in the light. It was going to be a heavy storm.

I put my head close to his and pointed down the slope. "I think that's where he stays, down there."

"In weather like this?" Officer Gainer whispered back.

"I know it doesn't seem likely." I smiled, thinking about my most recent visit to dreamland and the image of Joe playing three-card monte in the woods. "I've just got a hunch."

"Okay," he nodded. "That's good enough for me then." God love him.

We started slowly down the bank, trying not to make any noise.

The ground was already slippery from all the moisture in general, but the ice on the leaves was really making it hard to keep steady.

After we'd move about halfway down, I saw a flash of movement almost directly in front of us, about thirty yards ahead through the thick trees. Then a spark of light from the same direction caught the kid's attention too. He shot a look at me. I nodded.

We stopped. He pulled his gun and motioned for me to go right and that he'd go left. I nodded, and we moved.

As I got closer, I could see two figures. One was seated on a small crate or an overturned bucket or something. The other one was standing up, holding something in front of the seated figure.

Then the standing one flicked a lighter—the spark we'd seen before—and I could see that the one sitting down was Joepye. He looked to be crying, or maybe his face was just wet with the sleet. The other figure had his back to me, but I could see he was holding out a bottle, taunting Joe with it.

I'd lost sight of the kid, but I had to get closer in. I had to get a look at the other guy and hear what he was saying to Joe.

Just as I made it around a big sycamore, I heard Officer Gainer cuss loudly, followed instantly by his gun going off. I still couldn't see him, but I figured he'd slipped and fallen. There were lots of tricky little rocks and holes all over the bank, and it was slick as a slide. The guy standing in front of Joe turned wildly around in the direction of the noise, and I used the distraction to hustle in and get as close as I could to

Joe. I had it in mind to tackle the other guy and wrestle him to the ground.

But Joe saw me before I could get close enough to him, and he called out. "Flap! Help! She won't give me my wine back!"

The other guy spun around, still clutching the wine bottle in his hand, and it turned out it wasn't a guy at all. Even in the black of night I could see that it wasn't a guy.

It was Beth Dane.

35

BOX STEP

"You don't want that wine, Joe," I said when I'd re-covered my voice, which took a moment.

"Oh, yes, I do, Flap," he insisted. "I need a drink in the worst way in this world."

"Not this bottle, pal." I smiled at the girl. "This one's got rabies in it."

Just a guess, but it hit the mark. She set the bottle down on the ground—extremely carefully—and corked it hard.

Then: "How'd you know that?" She stared over her shoulder. "And who the hell is that over there shooting at me?" Sudden panic rising. "Is it my un-cle?"

"No, Beth." I tried to sound calm, staring at the ghost. "It's the police."

"He called the police? That son of a bitch, I'll wreck him! I'll spread his dirty little secrets all over the world!"

"He didn't get the police." I tried inching toward her. "The police got him. They already know his dirty little secrets."

"You did this!" She spun around to Joepye. "You geeky little *zip,* I'll kill you twice!"

"Joe didn't tell either." I was almost beside her. "I did."

She finally realized that I was almost on her, and she started to shift away and run, but the ground was worse than she'd expected, and she sloshed her way a few steps until she saw Officer Gainer stepping carefully her way with his pistol pointed at her.

"Damn!" she hollered at the top of her lungs. "Why does everything happen to me?"

"That's just about what your uncle said"—I smiled at her—"when we caught him."

She shot a look back my way, but her eyes were wild and unfocused. "Who the hell are *you?*"

Joe answered before I could. "That's Flap, Beth. Remember I told you about him?"

Now that I was up close to her, I could see that she was heavily conked. I was guessing speedballs, a zippy little injection of cocaine and heroin. The coke gives you enough bounce to stay alert so you can appreciate the skag and not nod off right away. It was a known cocktail of choice among some of the area's working girls.

She could barely focus on my face. "Oh. Right. You're Flap Tucker. Big deal. What do you want?"

Officer Gainer had made it down to our little party and was standing there staring at the girl.

"It's Beth Dane," was all he could say. Then he looked at me. "She's not dead."

"Doesn't look that way." I nodded his way, then turned back to her. "And I'll tell you what I want most in this world, Beth: I want some answers."

"To *what*?" She was just about to fall down. The panic and the drugs were colliding.

Where to start? "You hung those bodies. You and Joepye. You killed the girls and hung them up on a lamppost."

"Not me." She shook her head loosely "Joe did it all."

He stood. "I did not."

Like they were arguing about marbles.

Joe looked at me. "Honest to God, Flap. I didn't kill nobody."

I nodded. "You just hoisted them up the pole."

"Well." He shrugged. "Yeah . . ."

"He stole the germs"—Beth took a step in my direction—"and he helped me give it to them. And he did *all* the stuff at the police station."

I finally had to defer to Officer Gainer, who was obviously dying to comment.

"Mr. Tucker, you got to let me arrest these two, and we got to get them to Detective Huyne *right* now." His voice betrayed the surface of a deep, erupting excitement. "This is *so* big."

I took in a breath. "Okay, I guess you're right. But I'm not having Huyne spirit them off before I know what's what, so you can arrest them and give them their rights like you're supposed to, but you'll drive pretty slow after that, right?"

He considered, then nodded. "That's only fair."

Officer Dirt Gainer arrested the two lost souls, put them in handcuffs, and read Miranda rights, loud, from a printed card. I had to suggest that he get something secure to put the wine bottle in. Even though she had more or less admitted what was in it, we both knew it still had to be tested. I personally felt I needed some proof for my theory about Beth's feeding the third toxin, the rabies stuff, to Joepye: to keep him quiet permanently. Not to mention the fact that I certainly didn't want it floating around loose.

We all struggled getting back up the hill, which was nearly white with shaved ice by then, and there was all manner of slipping and sliding on our way to the prowler.

Joe and Beth took the back seat, and I rode shotgun. Seemed the official way to do things.

I waited in the car while Officer Gainer donned a surgical mask, and two pairs of gloves and went back down the hill with a serious containment bag to get what was left of the wine bottle and anything else he could find.

It took a little convincing from me that I would really be all right in the car with the other two. I'm not certain which of us he was worried about the most.

After he'd disappeared into the woods, I looked back at Beth. She was staring at the floor of the car.

"Beth?"

"Huh?" She seemed startled.

"Who was the first girl?"

"What?"

"If that wasn't you hanging up there the other night in your clothes, then who was it?"

She focused for a moment and squinted out fire at me through both eyes. "How should I know?" Snap to her left. "Ask him."

I tried to keep my voice calm. "And what did you mean when you said that about Joe here—speaking of Joe—doing something at the police station?"

"I don't know." She'd turned sullen in the blink of an eye.

Joe nudged her with his knee. "You might as well tell him; he'll find out anyhow." Whisper. "He's real smart."

She cracked out a laugh so sharp it could have cut bone. "Yeah. He's *real* smart. He thought that was me hung up there like a bunch of bananas."

"Isn't that what you wanted me to think?"

Her eyes met mine again, almost smiling. "You're not so smart. You didn't get half the clues. I wrote the notes on corny old computer paper, and you never got the connection. I named the bodies after dances, and you never found the goddamn Web site." She shook her head. "And you didn't even find my hotel room. How the hell do you make a living at this?"

"Luck, mostly." I looked at Joe. He was staring

out the window like we were taking him on a little ride in the country. "So, Joe . . . she was trying to kill you, you realize that? She had the rabies, the third thing you stole from CDC; it was in the wine bottle."

He kept staring. "I expect it was at that."

"Doesn't that make you . . . I don't know, mad or something?"

"At Beth?" He finally looked at me. "Naw. She's just doing what she has to do."

"Shut up," she told him.

"Look, it don't matter what I say now." He looked at her. "We're caught, darlin'. We're in a police car. That up there in the front seat, that's Flap Tucker. He's got us. He has this—how would you say?—*way* that lets him find out *everything*. He already knows what you did."

While I sat there wishing that what Joe had said were true, a couple of things came to me. I knew I only had a very little time before Dirt would be back and we'd go to the police station and Huyne would ask all the questions and I wouldn't find out anything.

"You knew Minnie," I said softly. "I know that much."

"So what?" she spit.

"So why'd you have to kill her? She wasn't involved in any of this."

"See?" Joe told Beth pointedly.

"I didn't kill *nobody*!" Her voice was jagged with hysteria.

"But you did know Minnie. I saw a photo of hers in your bedroom." Suddenly the rest of Beth's apartment was floating in my mind's eye again. "And there were some charcoal sketches at your place too." I nodded. "That's how you met Minnie. You posed for the life class at the College of Art—or maybe even at your apartment."

"*See?*" Joe's voice was nearly screeching.

"Shut up. So what? I posed. I know you can check that with the college. I posed. It was great money . . . just to *sit* there nekked." She stared at me. "That means absolutely nothing."

I went on. "So, anyway, you faked your death, then you had Joepye blackmail your uncle so that you could both have money—"

Joe interrupted. "But *I* was the one who told her we needed something to throw *you* off."

Beth chopped out a short laugh.

"Yeah"—I turned to Joe—"why did you get me involved in the first place?"

"Oh." He looked out the window. "I don't know."

I leaned back. Somehow Joe had known I would be involved in the deal and had decided to make the first move, a preemptive strike, or maybe that had even been Beth's idea. That would explain Joe's odd behavior that night and then his not even telling me that he knew Beth Dane. But why would I have been involved in the first place? What could possibly have connected me to this except for the fact that Joepye had gotten me up in the middle of the night and forced me to look at a dead girl swaying in the wind?

I was staring at Beth, wondering what I could do

to make her crack and give me the answers I wanted. But all I could think about, like the first time I'd seen her picture, was how much she looked like little Janey.

I only had a few seconds of *that* ricocheting around my brain before it actually hit something important and jogged loose the key image from my dream thing.

I saw a gallery, a long line of photos in a darkened hall. One of the images climbed out of the frame of the photograph and stole away, down the hall, laughing quietly. Then, a moment later, it brought another photo of another girl and hung it where the original had been, tossing away an empty frame. It was so mind-numbing that I couldn't really put it into coherent thoughts for a few more seconds.

"Jesus." I startled both Joepye and Beth. They were staring at me. I was staring back at them.

"Flap?" Joe's eyes were peering into mine.

"That's why you knew I'd eventually come to be involved in all this no matter what." I could barely form the words. "That first body"—I closed my eyes, and I could see it—"was Janey Finster."

36

FAITH

Before I even had a chance to swallow, Officer Gainer was slamming the lid down on the secure box in the trunk of the squad car.

"*Damn*, it's cold out there." He jumped in and cranked the car.

I turned back around in my seat, and I heard Joepye whisper to Beth, "I *told* you about Flap."

Beth didn't say anything.

I tried to make my voice sound nonchalant. "Say, Officer, would you mind just dropping me off back at Ms. Oglethorpe's house? Don't you think Detective Huyne and everybody would have gone home by now? I think I've had enough for tonight."

"I guess that would be a good idea." He nodded. "This is a police matter really."

"Yeah." I took in a deep breath and blew it out again. Might as well let the police in on the big secret. "You might just mention to Detective Huyne that the reason his stuff was burned in the park this evening was that all those files had Joe's fingerprints on them."

"What?" He nearly stopped the car.

"Isn't that right Joe?" I called to the back seat.

"Right as rain, Flap." He sounded almost happy.

"Joe switched the fingerprints on the first murdered girl while he was in the jailhouse. It really wasn't that hard for him—like picking a pocket, wasn't it, Joe?"

"Just that easy." He was content.

I managed a smile in Officer Gainer's direction. "I've seen how some of the guys at the station house have Joe fix things when he's in for the night—a Walkman here, a toaster-oven there. So he took advantage of the situation and switched the prints somehow."

"But—" The car slowed" "So who was the first girl?" Officer Gainer sounded more excited than anything else.

I was hoping my voice wouldn't come out funny when I told him. "Well, that's another little thing to tell Detective Huyne from me: That was Jane Finster." It was still hard for me to say.

"What?" The kid's eyes opened wide.

I turned a little to catch Joe out of the corner of my eye. "That's why Joe got me out of bed a couple of nights ago." More educated guessing. I looked him in the eye. "You'd overheard the cops talking about how they thought Mickey Nichols had killed Janey, and you knew Janey and I were friends, so you thought I might be involved already—because of *that*."

"That must be *exactly* what I thought." He rocked forward.

"Oh, my God!" Beth exploded. "He didn't know *dick*! He was too stupid to realize *anything* about what I had in mind. *I* got him to go fetch you. I told him how to get Janey's body out of the morgue. I arranged the fake cremation. I even had to put the spider juice in her tea myself. *Damn!*" She took a second to calm a little. "I had to find out if people would believe the body was mine. I couldn't very well get Nichols, or my uncle, out in the middle of the night, but Joe could get *you* on the pretense of your so-called work. If you didn't recognize that it was Finster, then I'd be cool. If you did, it would be Joe who got screwed, not me. Got that?"

"She's right, Flap." Joe leaned back, smiling. "I was too stupid to realize any of that."

But I looked at his face, and I saw the triumph there: He'd just gotten Beth to admit it was all her idea—in front of the police. He was staring out the window again, but that look never left his face, he just kept smiling.

I turned to Beth again. "Why Janey?" My voice sounded strained, even to me.

"That's right," she hissed. "Why Janey? Why'd she get everything and I get nothing? She got to dance all over town, she got invited to the big parties, she was everybody's girl." She broke our stare. "Why not me?"

I thought for a second then—I don't know exactly why—about the Beth Dane who could have been: somebody in the chorus of *The Nutcracker* every year, somebody in art school with Minnie Moran. Somebody whose family had watched out for her just a little.

After we swung by Dane's and saw that everybody had gone, and Dally's car was nowhere in sight, Officer Gainer dropped me off at Dally's house and roared away. Before I was even up on the steps, she had the door open.

I could see a fire in the fireplace, and I could smell dark coffee. I turned to watch the prowler pull away, then went to the door.

"Who was that in the cop car beside Joe?" she said. Then she got a look at my face. Must have been a sight. "My God, Flap, what is it?"

"In the car?" I told her, trying not to look her in the eye. "That's Beth Dane."

Dally dropped a silence heavier than an anvil.

I just went on. "She killed Janey Finster and Minnie Moran."

"Beth Dane?"

"Just let me come in and sit by the fire for a minute and warm up . . . if I can. Then I'll see if I can't unfold the details, okay?"

She just stood there.

All the details actually came out over the next few

days. Some of them came from me; some of them came from state-of-the-art interrogation techniques as practiced by Detective Burnish Huyne on Joepye Adder and Hepzibah Dane.

I guess you could say that it had all really started a few years back when Beth Dane had come to town. She was a tap dancer but wanted to study classical. She was going to be a ballerina. She was young, pretty, and willing to do almost anything. It hadn't taken long for her uncle to set her up with one of the less reputable escort agencies—to earn money for her dreams. I guess some people's idea of what the word *family* means is different from my own—but I digress. By the time Beth had realized what her uncle was doing, she was already turning tricks and "modeling" for the Internet, the site called "The Little Dancers."

She'd always wanted out, but she'd also wanted money.

Enter Janey Finster, who had it all. High-flying boyfriends, money, looks—everyone loved her. They'd met at parties like the one at Foggy's house on New Year's Eve, parties where Janey'd been a guest and Beth had been more or less the employee of a guest, usually. Beth had seen how everyone watched Janey when she danced: swinging up into the air, amazing everyone.

Beth was burned up with jealousy: Why Janey? Why not her? They even looked alike.

Joepye had actually met Beth at Dane's house. Joe really did do little odd jobs for Dane. When Beth saw him in the Midtown squad room one night after they'd both been arrested—ironically, she on account of her profession and he for his lack of profession—she'd struck up a conversation.

The idea really hadn't come completely together for her until she'd gone to see Minnie's show at the College of Art before the Christmas break. Minnie'd invited her after one of Beth's modeling sessions in Minnie's life class at the college.

And here's a tough part of the story for yours truly: Beth got all her ideas about how to hang the girls from a story about Gérard de Nerval that she'd overheard at the opening. Minnie had retold the item about his walking a lobster like a dog and then about his weird suicide—something Minnie had heard from me at her summer party.

Beth had killed Minnie partly so that their connection wouldn't be immediately obvious. That way Minnie wouldn't put two and two together when she heard about the particulars of the first murder only a few blocks away from where she lived. But mostly Minnie had died because Beth had decided that killing one person was a crime that was easy to trace. Setting up a serial killer, and one so weird that it scattered everybody's nerves—*that* was a great cover. Especially involving two such unconnected people, two such seemingly random targets. Not to mention that Beth had recently told the police in a moment of idle conversation that her favorite bedtime reading material was true crime books. She'd claimed to have read every book about Albert DeSalvo ever written. She'd asked the police if she could have her books—and her

Raggedy Ann doll. They were in a cheap hotel room, get this, under the name Gerri Nerval—just one more surreal clue that had gone unnoticed in the cold light of day.

But those notes pinned to the bodies had been Beth's proudest invention, her best clues, left just for me, as it turned out. She'd concocted the references to dances thinking they would be so obvious, partly because of Joepye's bragging about my eclectic reading habits, partly because they'd been written on arcane computer paper. Then I would discover Dane's Web site, and I would put two and two together, come to the conclusion that Dane was the murderer. Tying the notes and the toxins together had been the polish on the apple. She really had been, in her best moments, as bright as Dane had said she was.

She'd done it all to set up her uncle for her own murder. Partly to get out of the life her uncle had gotten her in, partly to blackmail him for lots of money, but mostly as cold revenge on the man who had ruined her chances for a life as a ballerina. It was brilliant. And it would have worked too.

The problem with it was that she'd done a lot of it under the assumption that I was as clever as Joepye had said I was. But I think we could all see how clever I had actually been.

Anyway, Dane had been released pending interstate pornography charges. Beth was on her way to being indicted for two homicides. Joe Adder was held as an accessory. Huyne even gave me an official police thank-you call.

When I told Mickey "The Pineapple" Nichols all this information, he just handed me an envelope with more hundred-dollar bills in it. He told me I'd done a good job. His only question was "Then whose ashes do I have in Janey's urn?" He hadn't taken them to Piedmont Park to sprinkle in the Botanical Garden. He'd kept them on his mantel.

I went to see Joepye in jail a few days later, to ask him about Mickey's urn, among other things. He told me he was scared of Mickey. "The ashes in that urn were just what was left after one of my hobo fires in the park, Flap. When I got Janey's body from the morgue? I just fixed the paperwork—like Beth told me—so that it looked like she'd already been sent to the crematorium. I delivered the fake urn there myself that night. When Mick finds that out—with everything else there is for him to be mad about—I'm afraid he might try and kill me."

I'd shaken my head. "Mickey is more reputation than actual behavior, Joe."

Then, the day after that, Dally and I were watching the local news and cooking dinner. We stopped our work because of the lead item. A police squad car— the one taking Beth Dane from the Midtown holding facility to the city lockup that morning—had blown up. Beth Dane was dead, but the officer driving the car had been called back inside seconds before the explosion and so had miraculously survived. The investigation was barely started, of course, but experts believed that there might have been an army surplus hand grenade involved.

I spent a lot of time trying to sort it all out, talking up a storm late at night with Dally, sitting beside her fireplace. For a change there was no wine involved. I wanted a completely clear head.

"What's *really* bothering you, Flap? Why can't you let this one go? I mean, you were close to Janey, I understand, but it's not just that. I can tell." She shifted a little closer to me on the couch. "Is it because you didn't recognize her when you saw her body?"

The fire was dying, and the room was dark and warm and orange.

"No. After it's all said and done," I told her, leaning into her shoulder, "would you like to know what really gets me?"

"I think that was my question, yes."

"Okay. Here goes." I steadied myself with a long breath. "All the things that should have been clues—a lot of them, anyway, like the Raggedy Ann doll, or the notes, for instance—which I could have used to deduce that Beth was still alive? Those clues meant nothing. Some of them I didn't even *find*, like the way Beth registered at the hotel."

"Maybe it's because they weren't real clues, Flap." She rolled out reasonably. "They were manufactured. They were phony. That's not how you work. You find the *real* clues. I'm not surprised you ignored the faked ones."

"But the thing that really had the biggest impact on

my figuring out what happened"—I kept on, brow wrinkled—"was that the girls were coming out of picture frames and the pictures were switched, and it's got me worried."

"Worried? I'm not sure I even understand how that image—"

"You know how I'm always saying there's nothing special about my little trick—"

"All the time you're saying this, yes." She was smiling, I could tell by the sound of her voice.

"And that it's all just a putting together of the picture puzzle pieces from the big picture: simple observation from the subconscious, nothing mystical about it . . . that sort of thing."

"I know the rant," she assured me.

"Then tell me this: What did I observe that could possibly have led me to know anything about Beth Dane's switching bodies and identities the way I saw in the thing?"

No answer.

I sat up. "Dally?"

"Yes?" She sat up too, peering into my eyes in the darkness, half amused, a little sleepy.

"See, I'm saying it didn't work the way it usually does, did it? First I couldn't do it at all; then I got what seems to be what they might call in the spiritual game insider information—stuff that I could not possibly have known."

"And?" The big shrug.

"What if there really is more to my little trick than meets the eye?" My face was nearly touching hers.

"Oh, I see." She moved even closer.

"Oh, you see *what*?" I could feel her ear touch my cheek. The light from the fire was nearly gone from the room.

"You're afraid"—her lips were touching my ear, and her voice was a sigh—"that you might actually become a man of some faith."

I turned, and I had only a split second to catch the look in those green eyes before she kissed me.

I always like to say that faith is nothing but experience, that you don't *know* something until you *do* it. But when you come across something outside the realm of your actual experience and it still has a profound effect on you, then you start to examine the whole concept of faith. Or I do, anyway.

And here are my conclusions after such an examination. Faith does not exist to move mountains. Mountains will eventually crumble into the sea all by themselves, so what's the point of moving them at all? Here are the reasons you really need faith: To get you through the day. To help you sleep at night. To ease your mind about the things you can't explain, to give you the occasional insight into the unknowable.

But most of all, you need faith to help you accept a kiss, when it's given to you, without right away asking all the wrong, stupid questions that would just mess the whole thing up.